No Good-Bye

Georgie Marie

ISBN: 1492276057
ISBN 13: 9781492276050
Library of Congress Control Number: 2013915985
CreateSpace Independent Publishing Platform
North Charleston, South Carolina

Preface

Gloria Madsen was not the average housewife. Her father said she was beautiful. A friend said she was absolutely "drop-dead gorgeous!" Another friend stated that Gloria looked like a movie star.

Gloria was in her early forties and just a few pounds overweight. Richard, her handsome husband, accused her of being afraid of her great beauty fading.

"You'll never have the shape you had when you were sixteen." He smirked. "You live in a dream world. When are you ever going to face reality?"

In reality Gloria was a romantic. At times her existence felt too mundane, and daydreaming was an escape.

When Dr. Benjamin Carter came into her life, her whole world changed. It was very real when he swept her off her feet and opened the door to heaven—an experience never to be forgotten.

Gloria always got what Gloria wanted. Or did she?

This book is dedicated to my wonderful children, who have the utmost faith in me.

Acknowledgements

First and foremost, I would like to thank my daughter, Charmaine, for her never-ending encouragement, inspiration, and tedious help proofreading, revising, and assembling all of my twenty-eight chapters. I would also like to thank her husband, Paul, for his patience while Charmaine assisted me in making my dream come true.

I would also like to thank my husband, Bob; my daughters, Bobbie and Jackie; my sons, Rick and Dominique; and my son-in-law, Terry, as well as the rest of my family and friends who believe in me.

Chapter 1

Talk Radio - January 1971

Gloria stood at the kitchen sink, lazily washing the breakfast dishes and wondering just what kind of a day it would be. Housework was really not her forte. The family had left for work and school. It was relaxing now.

She turned on the little portable radio that sat next to her prized aquarium. The brightly colored fish swam to the top, wanting to be fed. "Not yet, you little darlings!" Looking at them she muttered, "Gee, sometimes I think it would be nice to be a fish—no cares or anxieties in the world, just swimming around and around all day." She turned up the volume on the radio a bit.

KXYZ was airing a two-way talk show. People from all walks of life called in and would talk about a variety of subjects from politics to domestic problems.

Richard, Gloria's husband, had said, "People who listen to that garbage aren't too bright, and they don't have enough to do!"

She had retorted, "Well, I sure do learn a lot about politics and lots of other things too!"

The little radio came in loud and clear. It sounded like an echo chamber. That was different from what she had heard before.

"Here is your charming personality, Dr. Benjamin, or Dr. Ben—whatever you choose to call him," said the announcer. "He is your man."

"Good morning, ladies and gentlemen. This is Dr. Benjamin and you are listening to the *Ask Dr. Benjamin* radio show. I'm all yours for this hour...so please call in with your questions, problems, and anecdotes, or maybe even tell me about your favorite pet. I am always interested in a great recipe too."

Gloria had been listening to Dr. Benjamin for over a month. His voice was so extraordinary and different from any she had ever heard. It was amazingly sensual, stimulating, and magnetic.

"I may as well listen and see what he talks about today," she said. "As for his voice, I think my imagination has been working overtime. I must be dreaming, though."

The sun was streaming through the kitchen window. The new Austrian curtains that were hanging so beautifully caught the rays and predicted a beautiful day. Gloria thought *I am caught up on my housework pretty much. Maybe today I'll just relax in my recliner in the living room and enjoy my favorite person.*

Dr. Benjamin answered his first caller, who sounded like an elderly lady. "Ah, a young lady. What shall we talk about?"

"Well, I've lived alone for ten years, and I'll tell you it's no picnic. The lights go out, and something goes wrong with the furnace, and what can I do?"

"Oh, I'm on your side. I live alone. I know what it's like," Dr. Benjamin replied.

The caller said, "I've got wonderful neighbors, though. They come over and cut my lawn. Most of the time I can get help."

Dr. Benjamin uttered, "Um, that's very nice."

"Well, I'll tell you," the elderly woman went on, "it's a worry. Okay, now I'm going to hang up and listen to you on the radio. You tell me something good, all right?"

"I'll try."

"Okay."

"Hey, thanks for calling. Bye now." Dr. Benjamin added, "She's right. It's good to have friends and neighbors. I have counted myself extremely fortunate in some circumstances I have found myself in. I think my sight and possibly my life were saved by a downstairs neighbor who rescued me from some paint fumes, and another time he drove me to the medical center when I had a case of ptomaine poisoning. The whole thing revolves around communication and sharing. Without those, life is simply an empty shell. Not like one you pick up on the beach—there is no echo!"

Gloria was definitely intrigued by this communicastor (an opinion leader in the mass media community) and kept close to the radio. He was completely different from the others. His voice positively flowed with charisma. Maybe she would call him today. What should she talk about? She would have to think of a subject that would be interesting.

Gloria's mind would not function. The only thing that penetrated her brain was that sexy voice coming over the airwaves. All she could do now was day-dream. She closed her eyes and imagined things that would not possibly happen except in her dreams.

Back to reality. Gloria had almost dozed off. Wishful thinking would get her absolutely nowhere.

Dr. Benjamin laughed wickedly. "If you are of a mind, why not give me a jingle? We'll talk about it." Sighing, he continued, "Oh, what can you tell me?" Gloria listened intently as he continued speaking. "How many people have been to Morrison, Aspen, or Ft. Collins and know where the best eating places are located? I've had the marvelous opportunity of touring our beautiful, colorful Colorado, and if you can find a town I haven't been in, I'll give you a cancelled three-cent stamp or something. We can talk about that if you'd like, or we can talk about the Australian relative of the common earthworm, which ranges in length from four to eleven feet. This might come in handy next time you're doing a crossword puzzle."

Dr. Ben was definitely very different from anyone Gloria had ever listened to on the radio. The hour seemed to fly by. The commercials took up too much time. The phone calls were coming in one after the other. It wasn't exactly what Dr. Benjamin said but the delightful and sensual way the extraordinary tones of his voice flowed over the airwaves.

Dr. Benjamin was looking out the big glass window of the tiny radio station during the long commercial break—a necessary evil. "That lady has walked by here four or five times in the past ten minutes," he said. "I don't know what's happening, but if I'm not here tomorrow, why, you've been warned?" He gave a wicked laugh.

KXYZ was located in the middle of town. It was a busy section. The courthouse was nearby. People were constantly coming and going past the radio station.

Another caller was on the line. "Hello. Do you know anything about purebred dogs?"

"You just triggered a thought in my mind," said Dr. Benjamin. "I think maybe dog purists will call up and disagree, but it's been my good fortune to have mixed breeds every time I've had a dog, and I think they have worked out well. I don't know if there's something in AKC breeds or the registered kinds that make them temperamental sometimes or difficult to handle, but mixed breeds have always been very good to me and with me."

The caller went on, "We've had several different dogs through the years, and I've had these two for the last few years. Some were different in size and all, but, ah.... All I have to do is pick my scarf up or put on a sweater, and that dog figures I'm going to take him out. I don't have to say anything."

Dr. Benjamin and the lady caller were both laughing. She continued, "I'm trying to teach him to say 'out,' and he barks like he's saying, 'OUT!'"

"I've got mine trained to go out. I keep his chain on a slab of marble on a couple of blocks by my apartment door. All I have to do is rattle the chain on the slab of marble, and he's right there. He just knows."

"They know the sound or the movement. Now, I'm where there's a lot of traffic. I have to keep him tied up. Before I hang up, where are you from, Dr. Benjamin?"

"I was born in Georgia but have lived in several different states. I did teach at Kansas University for five years—psychology and history."

"Dr. Ben, you certainly have a good voice. I enjoy listening to you. Well, be good."

"I'll try." Dr. Benjamin and his caller both laughed.

"I'll talk to you again."

"Okay, thanks for calling. Bye-bye now." He went on, "Ah, what a delightful lady. Listeners, I want to emphasize this: if you're interested in topography or terrain, whatever, it's all there. All you have to do is go out and find it. It's immediately available. It really is. Someday I'll have to move to Salt Lake City. In the past couple of years, having traveled through the states, I think I can safely say with some authority that Utah has everything you can find in the other states in the continental United States. Utah has high mountains and meadows.

It has deserts and lush deciduous areas. If you want a complete countryside environment, you can find it in Utah. It's simply beautiful. Maybe I'll move there one of these days."

Gloria thought, *Humph. "One of these days" means none of these days.* That was one of the phrases she had learned to print when she had taken calligraphy lessons at the community school. It was one of many classes she had taken over the years.

The rules of Dr. Benjamin's show were to call in every other day, not every day, so other listeners would have a chance. Still, he didn't admonish Gloria even though she called him every day and was becoming addicted to his charming voice. Just listening to him became a ritual. Every radio in the house was turned on. If she was washing clothes in the basement, she would put her headphones on.

If Richard happened to be home, he would snap the radios off or to another station in utter disgust. He had no idea that his wife had fallen in love with Dr. Benjamin's voice. He just didn't think talk radio was worth anyone's time.

Gloria's thoughts plagued her. *I've heard of love at first sight but not love at first listen. I think I must be losing my marbles! He is not just an ordinary man because the words from his mouth are sweeter than honey, smoother than butter, and so sensual. He is A MAN WITH A MAGIC VOICE!*

Chapter 2

Another Day In Radio Land

The days simply flew by, and Gloria was in a good mood most of the time now. She did not yell or be argumentative as usual, although as a rule Richard was the perpetrator. He did things just to get a rise out of her. He always did! She had to learn not to react.

It was time for the program, and Gloria was fascinated. She couldn't miss it. Was it an obsession? By that time she was a regular caller. It seemed that Dr. Ben looked forward to her chatter and nonsense. Most callers did not really ask questions. They told him about their experiences. When Dr. Ben would ask, "Who is this calling?" she would say, "Bobette" and would change her voice somewhat. Why did she do this? She was sure the radio personalities used pseudonyms, and…there was a reason. A few of Richard's friends at work also listened to talk radio and would anxiously report to Richard whenever they happened to hear Gloria.

It was strange that she didn't hear them, though. She really did not know their voices and wondered, quite frankly, how they knew hers. Some of her friends did think she had kind of a Southern drawl.

"We heard your wife on the radio today!" Snicker, snicker. Richard would get furious! If his so-called friends were listening to the talk show, didn't that make them less efficient on the job? Were they goofing off? Were they stupid? Did they have too much time on their hands?

The radio was on. Dr. Ben was speaking. "Well, I was over at the City and County Building this morning, and I bumped into Dr. Burke, the director of the Health Department. After I had picked myself up, because you know he's a big man—when you bump into him, you bounce a lot—he told me he had a home-health hint, and I asked him if I could share it with my listeners. He said that short naps help prevent aging, especially when you take a nap while driving!"

Funny? Maybe. Gloria was on the line now. "Hola, Señor Ben, *como estas*?"

In a smooth, sexy voice came the reply: "Oh, *je suis bien, et vouz*?"

"You're too smart for me."

He laughed. "Well, you asked me in Spanish. I replied in French. Those are both Romance languages. I thought that was nice of me."

"Very good. Hey, when are you going to write your book of memoirs?"

"I'm…ah…a…. I'm too busy planning my past to get involved with that now," said Dr. Ben.

"You know, one time you did mention the fact that you were writing a book. I believed you."

"Yes. *How to Be Happy Though Married* is the tentative title."

"Listen, I looked up an old essay about dreams. I wrote it in school years ago. It has a lot of interesting things in it. If we have too many covers on, or if we don't have any, or just what position we're in all have bearings on our dreams."

"Hmm, I didn't realize that."

"Do you know what's aggravating, though?" Gloria asked.

"What?"

"Well, when you have a dream, and you want to analyze it, you find your dream book and get all excited, and then it isn't in there."

"Guess you can write your own then. Hey, I've got to go now. We're going to have some news."

"Okay. Good-bye," Said Gloria.

"Good-bye now."

The news was rather long. Another communicastor came on, so Gloria read the day's mail and did a few little chores. She missed the first part of the following conversation.

Dr. Ben was back on. "We've got Sharon on the line. Sharon, what's happening at your place?"

"Nothing much. I'd just like to compliment you on the way you're handling your program. My television has been out for the past two weeks, and I've been listening to you."

"Thanks...I think." He was trying to hold back his laughter.

"No, I mean it sincerely, and, ah, the lady who called you and gave you such a bad time a few minutes ago? I just don't agree with her. She's probably hung up on sex and probably has problems and is afraid to talk to anybody."

"Well, you know what I think?" Dr. Ben asked. "I felt like that last week, and anybody who gets that uptight has got to suffer from chronic irregularity too."

"Yeah, yeah, I think so. As far as your program being attractive to people, I think you're fairly interesting and informative. It's kind of interesting to hear what you and other people have to say."

"You're very kind to say that. I'm glad you called.'

"I haven't had any problems like that myself, except I wish my husband would stop smoking."

"That subject hasn't come up yet. I don't know why. A lot of people really object to smokers—especially heavy smokers."

"Well, it's mainly for his health," the caller said. "If it were just off and on, I wouldn't object, but I feel like the ladies who called in are frigid and things like that. A lot of times they are afraid to talk to neighbors or friends, but they can talk to you. So far you haven't given them any bad advice."

"I try not to. It's difficult, you know, just talking for a few minutes with people, but really that's the whole foundation of this program. Nobody listens to needs. The people who own this station are finding our program is getting better and better acceptance."

Gloria certainly did agree with that statement. She didn't know if Dr. Ben was a medical doctor or maybe a doctor of psychology. Either way he was sympathetic to people's problems and gave expert advice.

She began taping a lot of Dr. Ben's programs. They were informative and amusing at times. She adored his smooth and sexy voice, as did all the ladies who listened to him each day. In her opinion listening to him was better than going to a psychiatrist.

Another caller was on the line. "Hello, Dr. Ben. I've got an interesting story for you. It happened fifteen or twenty years ago. This fellow was going to Chicago and packed his bag, all ready to go. Earlier his wife had found a ladies' black nightgown in the bag. She took a close look at it and thought *What can I do?* She remembered she had some itching powder."

Dr. Ben laughed heartily.

"So she took the itching powder," the caller continued, "put on a rubber glove, and saturated the black lace nightgown."

"Mmm, uh-huh, yes."

"I don't know what happened. I don't want to bring it up, because she was very happy in her marriage. She didn't want to ruffle his feathers, but you know, it's been months and months, and he hasn't been back to Chicago."

Laughing wickedly, Dr. Ben replied, "She probably cancelled his credit cards."

"I thought you'd find that interesting."

"That's neat, yes."

"I have another story," said the caller. "This one was during the war, when things were hard to come by."

"Uh-huh."

"This one gal was going to Colorado University and wrote to the newspaper, which ran a Molly Mayfield thing. Her aunt had given her a pair of inflatable falsies—you know, you can inflate them to any size you want?"

Dr. Ben was laughing up a storm by this time.

"She went out with this fellow," the caller continued, "and they were getting serious. You know what's coming?"

"He decided he would really like to—"

"Yes. He decided to pin her, and the falsies went zoosh."

Dr. Ben made a whistling noise.

"She says he got the funniest look on his face," said the caller. "That was three weeks ago, and she hasn't seen him since!"

"Can't imagine why! Hey caller, I'm out of time now."

"I can appreciate that, but I thought you'd like these stories. I love these poetic type of jokes."

"It's a nice way to end the week."

"Have a very pleasant weekend."

"You too, and we do have to cut out now. This is the voice of KXYZ news radio. KXYZ is the radio station that listens to people and cares. Be kind, thoughtful, and considerate. That's love—something most of us will not experience!"

Chapter 3

An Unusual Day

Gloria had developed a different attitude toward life since she had started listening to talk radio. She decided to take more interest in politics, perhaps to impress Dr. Ben. She kept the station tuned in all day and paid attention to the news. What was happening to her? Gloria even skipped her beloved soap opera, *Days of Our Lives.*

Dr. Ben was certainly amazing and gaining more admirers every day. His smooth, mesmerizing voice enchanted his audience, especially the ladies.

Tomorrow would be Valentine's Day. Gloria had something for Richard: a cute little, fuzzy white cat. When the paw was pressed, it said, "I love you, I love you." Would he like it? Maybe not. He no doubt would want to give it to one of their grandchildren.

David, the youngest of their children, was just getting out of bed. The rest of the family was gone for the day.

"Mom, I need to make a Valentine box for school," David said.

"Why in the world didn't you tell me before now?" Gloria asked.

"Sorry, I just forgot."

"It's a good thing it's still early. It won't be pancakes for breakfast, though. You'll have to be satisfied with grapefruit and toast—and milk, of course. Don't take too long to get ready for school. You can help make your Valentine box."

Gloria managed to find an old cigar box, some red crepe paper, ribbon, and little cupid stickers. It didn't take long at all to decorate it. They both worked on it and covered the cigar box first with the crepe paper. To their surprise it turned out very well. Gloria had quite the artistic knack; her children had the same quality.

Luckily David had signed his Valentines and put them in their little envelopes a few days earlier. He very carefully put them in the pretty box they had made.

"Gee, Mom, thanks," he said.

"You're welcome. Now get to school. It's time to go. Oh my, you didn't get to watch *Underdog* on TV this morning."

"Oh, my favorite. That's okay, though."

Gloria kissed her son good-bye as he went out the door with his lunch and Valentine box. The school was only a block and a half away.

The kitchen table was a mess and needed clearing. Suddenly an idea popped into Gloria's head. Under her breath she muttered, "I'm going to make Dr. Ben a Valentine!" She had a lot of ideas, some original and some from the greeting cards she had studied diligently at a Hallmark store recently. She always took notes and drew quick sketches right there in the store if she saw something interesting. Nobody seemed to notice.

What luck, a piece of white cardboard was still there on her kitchen table. She quickly sketched a shapely lady on it, clad in a scanty costume, and covered the body with astrological symbols. Astrology always lingered on her mind. She was well informed on the subject thanks to one of the many classes she had taken over the years. Her illustration of the lady was original. She did copy a verse, though, which she had read at a store recently. So on the front of Gloria's card was the shapely lady saying, "I'm going to give you something I've never given you before!" When the card was opened, it read, "This card, of course, you DREAMER!"

Gloria colored the illustration and even put gold glitter on the woman's costume. She held the card in her hand and admired it. It was good...even exceptional. Instead of signing her name, she drew her astrological symbol, Libra, and filled it in with the gold glitter too.

Gloria was feeling a sense of exuberance and thought this was a day to be remembered. Luckily she was able to find a large envelope to fit the card and addressed it to Dr. Benjamin Carter at the radio station's address. She put two postage stamps on it just in case it weighed over the limit.

She literally jumped into her clothes, put on a pair of sneakers, and ran a brush through her curly hair. What a change! She usually didn't get dressed so soon. The mailbox was two blocks away and uphill. By the time Gloria got there, she was huffing and puffing. She could just hear Richard saying, "You're out of shape. You need to lose weight!" Yes, the truth did hurt. Maybe things would change. It was a positive thought.

Gloria was pumped. Today she did not envy the fish in the aquarium and was glad to be herself, a human being.

There was a loud noise outside. It was the beautiful blue jay atop the evergreen tree who visited every morning. He was gorgeous in his array of blue and white feathers and was jabbering up a storm. Another blue jay flew up beside him. They were chirping at one another heatedly, maybe in a lover's spat.

"I wonder what they are saying to one another," Gloria said under her breath.

It was time for her to get off cloud nine and get started on the usual routine. It was surprising how much she could accomplish when she was in a positive mood. Every radio in the house was turned on. Sometimes the tape recorder was on. In fact Gloria had several tapes she had previously recorded. Now and then, when she was alone, she would replay them, always marveling at Dr. Ben's voice.

It was that time again. The first caller was on the air. "Good morning, Dr. Ben. I want to talk about the prison smoking ban in Folsom, California."

"Well...ah...go right ahead. We should have a serious subject now and then."

"All the inmates will be forbidden to smoke."

"Yes," answered Dr. Ben. "They have always been supplied with cigarettes and matches. I think smoking bans in prisons are wrongheaded and create more problems than the do-gooders who impose them can ever imagine. I have heard through the grapevine that there is no such thing as a total ban on smoking in prisons. Folks always find something to take. That is my humble opinion."

"That doesn't sound too hopeful, Dr. Ben. Do you mind if I ask you another question that is practically the same subject?"

"Okay, but make it short. I have another caller on the line."

"How do you feel about no more Viagra for sex offenders?"

"From what I've read through the years, those who commit sex offenses are not after the sex itself but seeking power over their victims. I'm also aware that therapists and other treatment folks are quite divided on this and on the best way of treating people."

"Thanks for your input, Dr. Ben. Good-bye now."

"Bye. We have another caller on the line. Hello-oh, and who do we have on the line?"

"This is Bobette." Gloria used that name now when she talked on the air, and she changed her voice somewhat. Richard's spies could go fly a kite now! "I have a question for you since the subjects are so serious today."

"Okay, Bobette, go ahead."

"What about the continuing poverty in Africa?"

Dr. Ben seemed somewhat astonished by the question. He was completely unaware of her decision to be informed on current events. However, his answer was immediate. "Absent the government at the top, no amount of aid from any source will alleviate African poverty. As long as BushCo continues to obey the Christofascists he's surrounded himself with, there will never be any meaningful program of public health education, family planning education, or even basic children's education. Africa is too rich a continent for US oligarchies to allow any improvement in the lives of its people."

"Thank you so much, Dr. Ben. I'll just have to concentrate on your answer. Have a good day."

Gloria was astounded by all Dr. Ben's knowledge and simply didn't know how to continue or respond. His convictions blew the wind out of her sails. Today he sounded as though he were a walking encyclopedia. She didn't digest his answer, just kept hearing the sound of his charming voice that captivated her senses. She wondered about his looks. Was he the handsome creature she saw in her mind, or was he ugly as sin? Her imagination was out of control. How could she concentrate on world affairs or politics? She couldn't—not now!

Gloria always had household duties to keep her busy. Raising five children, with four still at home, was more than a task; it was a lifetime commitment. The children ranged in age, one was married with children, two were in high school, one was in junior high, and one was in elementary school. Gloria was an only child and had always wanted to have six children. Five children were quite enough in this day and age; however.

This day had been most unusual. Sending the risqué Valentine to Dr. Ben was still milling around in her mind. Maybe she shouldn't have been so forward.... Maybe, maybe, maybe! Gloria thought this Valentine was juvenile. When she went to bed that night, her actions kept running through her mind. "Oh my goodness. What will Dr. Ben think?"

Gloria just couldn't wait until tomorrow!

Chapter 4

Que Sera, Sera

It was Valentine's Day. What would the day bring? Things were quiet on the home front now. Richard had left for work; the kids were at school. Thoughts kept running through Gloria's mind. *Would the Valentine reach Dr. Ben?* It was a known fact that at times the mail was slow or never reached its destination. The main issue in her mind kept repeating like a phonograph needle stuck in a groove: *what would Dr. Ben think, and just how would he react?*

Time seemed to stand still. The waiting was nerve-wracking. There were plenty of chores to be done this morning, but housework took second place today.

At last, at last, the clock ticked to 10:00 a.m. Gloria slipped into her easy chair, the recliner that was so comfortable. The volume of the radio was rather high. She heard a few refrains of a sweet song, and then it was time for Gloria to enjoy her favorite pastime: talk radio with Dr. Ben.

"This is KXYZ, two-way talk radio in Mountain America. The opinions expressed on two-way talk radio are those of the callers and the communicastors, who do not represent approval by this station management or our advertisers." Dr. Ben's voice was loud and clear. He continued, "Good morning, ladies and gentlemen….Ah…ah, I presume there are some gentlemen in the audience." His laugh was sly. "What's on the agenda today? It's your choice. We can talk about toenail fungus or why your marriage isn't heavenly. Mm…callers, where are you?"

Ben's voice was as smooth and sexy as ever, but good golly Molly, why didn't he mention Valentine's Day or how it got started? Didn't he receive the big Valentine that was sent to him by his secret admirer?

"Yes, yes, I have a caller on the line," he said. "Who is this?"

"This is Matthew."

"Oh, you called the other day?"

"I did, Dr. Ben, but…today I want to talk about men!"

"Men? What about men?"

"Have you noticed how men are changing these days?"

"Yes, Matthew, I have noticed how men are changing."

Matthew was getting riled. "You know, there's not many real men left…not many male chauvinists!"

"Male chauvinists, huh?"

"Yes, Dr. Ben. I consider, oh, maybe truck drivers, ah, rodeo people, coal miners. Those are real men. They can do a good day's work. They are chauvinists—real men. We've all turned into a push-button society, and women just don't care for the soft male anymore. Men today can't do a good eight hours' work."

"Uh-huh." Dr. Ben was letting the caller go on and on.

"A woman likes a man who comes up and grabs her by the waist with a strong arm and pulls her toward him, and she feels muscle!"

Dr. Ben put in his two cents. "Come here, baby, and give me a kiss!"

"Yeah, kind of Clark Gable-like. That's what a woman wants these days. We'll never go back, and I think we should. I think we've lost it!"

Dr. Ben and the caller both laughed at this statement.

"Like I told you, Matthew, you can hang up this phone and disappear with amity. I have to sit here for another hour, and…ah…I'm not going to get stuck with this anymore. Did you hear that lady yesterday? She was on a tirade and called me a chauvinist!"

"Dr. Ben, I'd be proud to be called a chauvinist. I sure would be!"

Both of them laughed heartily.

Matthew went on talking. "I'm going to have lapel pins made up that say, 'I'm a chauvinist. Do you want to talk about it, babe?' The lapel pins would be in the shape of a pig. Yeah, man, in the shape of a pig. We should be proud to be chauvinists. Yeah, that's what we need. We need more chauvinists!"

"Okay, I'll tell you what. If you have those pins made up, I'll try to give them away on the air, and let's just see how many men we have come out of the closet—closet chauvinists."

"Dr. Ben, you know there are different degrees of chauvinists?"

"Oh, you don't say."

"My father was in the first degree. He was a true chauvinist. But the men of today are not like the men of yesterday, and…we're losing it, and if we don't get back, we'll be completely lost!"

Dr. Ben interjected, "We've abandoned our position of leadership, huh?"

"Right! The problem is women want equal rights. That's fine, but as you and I know, you give a woman equality, and she wants more than that. She won't stay at that level, and pretty soon we're being subservient males to the dominant female!"

"Right you are, and that's what's destroying marriages."

"A woman wants a man who's a man, not a sniveling…a sniveling…what do I want to say?"

"Well, Matthew, they want a John Wayne or Clark Gable. They want a man!"

"Dr. Ben, a woman needs a man she can look up to. Somebody who's stable, and during a crisis she can go to him and lean on him. These are my thoughts for the day. There'd be less divorces if there were more real men!"

"Matthew, thanks for stirring up a hornet's nest. I hope I still have a job tomorrow. Bye-bye now."

"Bye. I'll call again."

Another caller was on the line. "Hello, caller," said Dr. Ben, "and who do we have on the line now?"

"Bon swah."

"What?"

"Oh, bon soir or however you say it!"

Dr. Ben let out a big laugh.

"Dr. Ben, I've caught your hearty laugh, and it's quite contagious!"

"Oh, I have an infectious disease. Ha ha!"

"Not to change the subject, but have you ever had a Denver sandwich?"

'Yes, I have, and they are good."

"They are sold everywhere. The main reason for this call is I just want you to know how much I appreciate your program, and...and...wow, your voice is the nicest I've ever heard!"

"Thank you. I try. Bye now. Call again. That was a short call."

Gloria was about to give up hoping to hear anything about Valentine's Day. Her Valentine probably got lost in the mail. She kept relaxing in her easy chair and was enjoying another cup of coffee.

Dr. Ben's voice came through loud and strong. "Callers, this is the electronic soapbox where you can air your views. Let's hit the phones again. This is two-way radio, and you're on KXYZ, the station that listens to you and cares."

A caller came on. "Hello. Happy Valentine's Day!"

"Thanks a lot. Is this...ah...Bobette?"

"Is this who?" the caller asked.

Sounding disappointed, Dr. Ben said, "It's not Bobette."

"No...ah...ah," the caller stammered.

"Well, Happy Valentine's Day to you too."

"Ah...ah...uh, do you have a sweetheart?"

With a subtle laugh, Dr. Ben replied, "No, but...uh...there's a lady who listens fairly frequently, and she sent me a lovely, lovely Valentine. It's a little handmade job with astrological signs on it, with a rather cute message on it.... And I really thought she might—"

The caller interrupted before his sentence was finished. "That's nice. Dr. Ben, I just wanted to wish you a happy Valentine's Day, and I'll call you again soon."

"Oh, you're a sweetheart. Good-bye now."

By then Gloria—Bobette—was in a good mood. The waiting had been worthwhile. She hadn't listened to all of the calls, but it was time for the program to end.

"I'll be here tomorrow, same time, same station," said Dr. Ben. "I just want to mention again the lovely Valentine that Bobette sent me, and I thank her for it." His last words were so suave and sexy. "I've got to meet Bobette sometime!"

Chapter 5

Another Homemade Card

Gloria just couldn't believe the words Dr. Ben had actually uttered yesterday on his program: "I've got to meet Bobette sometime!" This thought had never, in all reality, entered her mind. She was just happy to hear him talk every weekday and was quite fascinated by his knowledge and command of the English language. His voice was so delightful that it just gave her strange little tingles all over. Gloria had never heard a voice as wonderful as Dr. Ben's.

The advice he gave to his callers was so good. One day, on the air, Gloria told him he gave better advice than a psychiatrist, and it was completely free—the callers didn't have to pay for it. Dr. Ben was amused. She had added, "Why, it's better than getting a hormone shot!"

It was true that Gloria's (or Bobette's) praise sent Dr. Ben on an ego trip. After talking with her or reading parts of her letter, he would purr, "Delightful lady" and laugh his wicked and wonderful chuckle.

Gloria never told Dr. Ben that just hearing his voice made her legs go weak and quiver; it was almost orgasmic. He was positively captivating. This was ridiculous and incredible. An adult woman should not have a teenage crush on a person she had never seen and didn't really know

The days flew by. Gloria was content to listen to Dr. Ben every day. The idea of meeting him was definitely an impossibility. She was a married woman and loved her husband and children to the ninth degree. Jeopardize her position in life? Never! But in her thoughts, Dr. Ben was her Prince Charming. Her imagination ran wild and knew no end. It was tremendous. Richard always told her she was a dreamer and she should face reality. Gloria retaliated by telling him she had read that in order to be a good author, one should have a great imagination!

The idea did enter her head, more than once, that she should write a romance novel or a how-to book. There were numerous things Gloria had learned to do in her older years. In fact she considered herself a late bloomer. She had taken many classes over the years just for entertainment. She had even taken astrology—one of her favorite subjects—at Colorado University as well as creative writing. It had seemed the teacher was more interested in playing his guitar and singing to his students than actually teaching them anything. He should have been reported to the school board.

Gloria and her daughter, Clarissa, took belly dancing lessons together. It was so much fun. Gloria was the oldest student in the class. What Gloria didn't learn at the lesson, her daughter taught her at home later. One of Gloria's dear friends, Susan, called her Wonder Woman. What a compliment! That was when Gloria had learned to ride a Jet Ski right off the bat. The friend had said Gloria could do anything.

If Gloria telephoned this friend at work, the secretary would say, "May I ask who is calling?"

"This is Wonder Woman!" Gloria would reply.

The secretary would stutter, "Who? Who?"

"This is Wonder Woman, and Susan knows me."

Gloria would be promptly connected. Many a laugh was had over this.

Although Gloria was a housewife, she was not just a plain-Jane, ordinary housewife. She definitely had a very high opinion of herself. Don't psychology books recommend loving yourself?

The sun was shining brilliantly. It lit up part of the kitchen. It made the atmosphere cheery and radiated on the calendar hanging on the wall. February stood out in bold black letters. Then, a bit down, were the red letters: "George Washington, February 22." They were inviting. An idea immediately popped into Gloria's mind. Why not make Dr. Ben a George Washington card? She didn't remember ever seeing a George Washington card. This could be original. It was a sure thing that nobody else would send that kind of card to Dr. Ben!

It was about time for the talk-radio show to come on. Gloria would listen to Dr. Ben and create the card simultaneously, thus killing two birds with one stone. First a cup of coffee was poured; then a paper plate and colored pencils were taken out of a nearby kitchen drawer. This endeavor would be such fun. The family did not need to know of this indiscretion. Wasn't it harmless?

The newspaper was on the table. There was a big picture of George Washington advertising a huge sale at Sears Department store. What luck having that nice picture right in front of her face! Although she was pretty good at drawing, this would be of such help and save time also. The colored pencils, magic markers, and big box of metallic pens were just waiting to be used.

George Washington was drawn in a few minutes. The colored pencils made him stand out. Good thing there were white pencils to fill in the white hair. The card was beginning to take shape. With bright, bold red letters, Gloria printed, "GREETINGS, FELICITATIONS, AND SALUTATIONS ON GEORGE WASHINGTON'S BIRTHDAY" around the paper plate. The card was beginning to look pretty good. Gloria turned the paper plate over and drew a funny lady. That wasn't enough. It needed something else. A poem—yes, something kind of quirky that would tell Dr. Ben how much he was admired. Gloria even admitted to him in the poem that she just couldn't get him off her mind.

The card was almost finished but not quite. It needed something to embellish it. Gloria opened a drawer in her sewing table and found some bright-red yarn and a large needle. These would add the finishing touch to her masterpiece. She put decorative stitches all around the edge of the paper plate and then tied a big, red bow on the front where George Washington was drawn. The card looked almost professional. Gloria's efforts had paid off.

George Washington's birthday was a few days away. Gloria stashed the big card away in a safe place where it wouldn't be seen and sat down to have a relaxing cup of coffee before cleaning up the evidence. She hadn't been concentrating on the callers' conversations with the famous man of her dreams on the radio. Now she could settle down and give her full attention to his every word while drinking her last cup of coffee.

A caller was talking. "I've been listening to you this morning for the first time ever, and I've had some laughs." Dr. Ben and the caller both laughed heartily. The caller continued, "Well, really, you remind me of someone I knew a long time ago, and...ah...and you just made my day!"

Dr. Ben answered in his mesmerizing voice, "I think we were lovers four thousand years ago, you and I."

"Do you believe that?"

"Sure!"

"So do I. I've enjoyed your program so much. I usually go somewhere, but today I can't get out, and…and…ah…I'm sure glad I stayed home and got to listen to you."

"Hey, love, my life has been so empty, and it's only because you've not been listening."

"Oh dear, that makes my day all over again!"

Dr. Ben and the caller both laughed again.

The caller added, "You were talking about lost dogs some time ago. Well, I have a little poodle that I simply adore, and, ah…. I feel so terribly sorry for that little dog who is lost, and I hope his owner finds him today. But back to your program. I'm sure everybody is happy listening to you. I know I certainly enjoyed this hour and get a kick out of your humor. To tell the truth, I'm a little bit crazy myself."

Dr. Ben gave a big sigh. "How many times can I fall in love this morning? So many nice ladies call me."

The caller kept on. "Isn't it great? You are so lucky!"

"Yeah, but I have to go home alone. The only one there is my dog."

"Well, Dr. Ben, I just don't know what to tell you, but…but…you be sure to be on the air tomorrow."

"Ah, I hope so, but that's up to the management team."

"I've listened to this station for many years and don't know why I haven't heard you before, but you—you are fun! I certainly enjoy your program."

"You are so kind. You really are. Call me again."

"Oh, I will for sure."

The hour had passed so quickly. It was quiet now, but the telephone disturbed the peace, ringing loudly. Gloria answered, "Hello."

A nasty voice came through. "Are you the lady who turns the tricks?"

Chapter 6

The Nasty Phone Call

Gloria was quite shaken. That phone call had been considerably upsetting. She knew where it could have come from: the talk-radio station, KXYZ. In a moment of stupidity several days ago, she had called the station when Dr. Ben was not on the air but possibly there. She gave her telephone number to the man answering the phone and asked if he would give it to Dr. Ben. Oh, what a dumb thing to do! Gloria, later in the day, called Dr. Ben at the radio station almost crying. He assured her he would straighten the matter out. He was very concerned. He had asked Gloria for her phone number some time ago, but she had been afraid to give it to him. It would not have served any purpose. She was true to Richard and always had been. As far as she knew, he had been faithful also. This idolizing Dr. Ben was just a housewife's pure fictional fantasy. Whatever possessed her should be extinguished!

Gloria completely forgot about the George Washington card and did not mail it until much later in the day. It would still get there the next day, so no worry. The last mail pickup at the post office was at 6:00 p.m.

The next day did not go well. Richard was getting ready for work, and he couldn't find his favorite socks. He yelled at Gloria, "Can't you even find time to wash my socks?"

"Richard, for heaven's sake, you have a dozen pairs in your drawer that would match your slacks. Would you please be quiet? The kids aren't up yet."

The kids were used to their mom and dad bickering over trifles and didn't consider it a big deal. It had always been that way and probably would never change. Sad but true!

Later, it was almost time for the radio program. Richard and the kids were gone for the day. Things would settle down and get back to normal and not be so stressful. Gloria's brain had stopped churning. She remembered something she'd read recently: "You know the leading cause of stress? Reality!"

"That's for darn sure!" she agreed.

The radio interrupted the silence and Gloria's train of thought. Every radio in the entire house was on. Right on time Dr. Ben's voice was heard loud and clear—that magical voice. There were just not enough adjectives to describe his beautiful voice.

"Good morning, faithful listeners. It's a beautiful day outside. What shall we talk about today? The gorgeous sunset we had last night, current events, or how to avoid old age? It's up to you. Oh, before we get started, I want to tell you… ah…it seems we had a prank call to one of our listeners yesterday—a nasty one. We have not found the culprit but do apologize for the grief it caused."

It was purposely not mentioned that the call had to come from the radio station!

"All right. Now that the air has been cleared, I'm ready for callers. In the meantime, if you have problems or wishes or, ah, concerns, or bad breath, ulcers, or whatever, please feel free to call here. I'll give you the opportunity to vent or to get stuff off your mind."

"Hello, Dr. Ben," said the first caller.

"Hello there. What's on your mind today?"

"Oh, I really can't tell you. Not today anyway."

"Yes, you can. I'm listening."

"Some other time. Right now I would like you to give me your recipe for pork chop stew. You gave it a few days ago, but I didn't get all of it. Would you, pretty please, repeat it?"

"I'd be glad to. Now, ah, everybody who wants this great recipe, get out your pen and paper. Here goes. Pork chop stew. Two cans of any kind of cream soup—cream of asparagus, cream of celery, whatever you have, and you throw it cold into a skillet and then smear it around all over the bottom with a pork chop. Then lay however many pork chops you want to cook in there on top of the cold soup and add, ah, celery, peppers, potatoes, carrots, and stuff like that. Then put the second can of soup on top and add all kinds of seasonings, oh, like a bay leaf, maybe a dash of sage, whatever you like. Put it on medium heat, and let it simmer for two hours, and I guarantee you will not have to use a knife on the pork chops." Dr. Ben spoke with conviction.

"Oh, thank you so much, Dr. Ben. I'm going to use your recipe today. My family will love it, I know. Bye now."

"We have another caller on the line."

"Dr. Ben, I can vouch for that recipe. My husband said those were the best pork chops he had ever tasted."

"Thank you, young lady. I'll take compliments any time I can get them," said Dr. Ben with his charming voice and infectious laugh.

"I have a suggestion, though," the caller said.

"Okay, what is it?'

"Buy a Crock-Pot. I bought one recently, and it's the answer to a maiden's prayer—also a bachelor's."

Dr. Ben laughed at this statement. "Yes, yes, go on."

"You can use it on low for ten hours. If you're home and want to hurry it up, you can use it on high for five hours, and…and…it's just perfect."

Dr. Ben said, "We, ah, we all chipped in recently…. A young lady in the office got married, and the secretary went out and got her a Crock-Pot. I looked at it and thought, *By golly, that is something I ought to have.*

"Well, I bought mine because they are highly recommended by so many people, and if you watch the specials, sometimes you can get them at a good price. I'm enjoying your program while I'm ironing. Carry on, Dr. Ben. I'll be listening."

"That was a delightful lady. Kind people—that is what two-way talk radio is all about. People just checking in and sharing things and what have you. Not to change the subject right now, but…has everybody forgotten that today is George Washington's birthday? I received a big George Birthington's Washday card from Bobette."

Dr. Ben did like to twist words around!

"She drew a picture of George Washington on a paper plate. What a lady. I am delighted to receive this special card, and I am going to hang it up on my living room wall. As a matter of fact, and this is true, this is the very first George Washington card I have ever received." He made a great to-do over it and repeated several times how much he appreciated the lovely card made from a paper plate and with so much originality and with all the frills.

Gloria had not called in today. When she heard Dr. Ben oohing and ahhing over the greeting card, her depression over that awful phone call disappeared instantly. She felt a surge of anxiety...of euphoria, of...what was it? She had not experienced this feeling, whatever it was, in a long, long time. She felt *alive*! Gloria wanted to call him right then and there, but what would she say?

I'd better wait 'til tomorrow when my mind isn't so twitterpated, and I can carry on an intelligent conversation, she thought.

Gloria had written down Dr. Ben's pork chop stew recipe the first time he had given it on the air. She tried it, and it met the approval of her entire family—even Richard. Dr. Ben knew a lot about cooking. His listeners were quite interested in his recipes and great cooking tips. He also talked a lot about the flowers he had planted last year; he was waiting for them to show signs of appearing if spring would just cooperate. Mother Nature would have to favor him. He seemed to be very knowledgeable about gardening among other things.

Another quality that Gloria admired in Dr. Ben was his vocabulary. It was tremendous. She would take notes on his words and learn the exact meanings. She hoped to impress him. She knew what she would say to him when the occasion arose. It was something her father had taught her when she was a little girl, and she had never forgotten it: "In promulgating esoteric opinions or articulating superficial sentimentalities, it is always well to beware of platitudinous ponderosities." What a mouthful of big words. Gloria loved big words and often said this little phrase now, even in her present age. Her family hated to hear it. They weren't impressed, but some of her associates were. At the end of the phrase, she would say, "Don't you think so?" She taught this to one of her daughters and two grandchildren. Her grandson had memorized it in fifteen minutes. Gloria had never known the origin of this saying. She wished she had asked her father while he was still alive.

Today's radio program was almost over. Gloria had taped it and would listen to it later. She hadn't given it her undivided attention today, but she was enthralled that Dr. Ben liked her George Washington card so much. What would she do next? It was a mystery to her what she had done already—acting like a teenage girl and having this infatuation with a man she didn't know and had never seen. She would think of something, but what?

Chapter 7

Reality

Actually there was absolutely nothing Gloria should have done about her juvenile adoration for Dr. Ben. The sensible thing to do was just to listen to him and be satisfied with the pleasure of hearing his voice and extraordinary laugh. She did record many of his programs and would listen to them when the family was not at home.

Gloria wrote letters to Dr. Ben often, commenting on his program, the bothersome commercials, what was likeable, and how much she enjoyed his show. He would tell the listeners about her letters and describe her beautiful golden penmanship, the perfumed stationery, and the sealing wax on the back of the envelope that said "LIBRA" and had a picture of the scales, the symbol of the astrological sign. He loved the rustic stationery. He invited his listeners to write to him, saying that he welcomed letters.

Several months flew by, and Dr. Ben was becoming more popular than ever. It was astounding. Gloria managed to call him on his program every day although that broke the rule, which was to call only every other day. Dr. Ben was always courteous to her and the others. He was never rude or cut off a caller as some other communicastors did—unless it was a crank call or some-one was swearing.

As a rule Dr. Ben was informative and funny. One day the callers seemed to have disappeared or gone on vacation. He had to ad-lib, but he was not at a loss for words. "The sportscast is coming on in a moment, but if you have problems, wishes, concerns, bad breath…ah, or ulcers or whatever, feel free to call KXYZ. Quite possibly we can air them, ah, perk you up, ah, give you an opportunity to vent or to—oh, get stuff off your mind, whichever is more appropriate."

The sports news didn't last too long—still no callers.

Dr. Ben sighed. "Well, sometimes I watch the people walking by. You know I have a huge glass window here. Some people walk by and flip a peace sign at me." He laughed. "Or half of one! But I say smile; it's a good thing. The world needs more smiles. Hey, not to change the subject, but do you know that the word *gopher* comes from the French word *gaufre*, meaning "welcome" or "honeycomb," an apparent illusion to the tunnels the animal makes?"

Laughing, Dr. Ben continued, "Did you know I'm just a bottomless pit of useless information. Uh-oh, a young girl just walked by and blew me a kiss. That makes my day! Whoa there.... Where are my fun-seeker callers?"

The phones were not ringing. The silence was deafening. Dr. Ben rambled on.

"It's a lovely, sunshiny day. Perhaps this should be a potpourri day with the topic being fires, explosions, or reactions to crises."

Finally somebody decided to call. "Where is everybody today?" he said.

Dr. Ben replied, "This hasn't happened before. Hope the station doesn't decide to replace me!"

"No chance of that, my man. You are the best communicastor who's ever been on KXYZ!"

"You're kind, sir. I appreciate it. What's on your mind today?"

"Dr. Ben, I've got the worst case of eczema, and...and...I just don't know what in the world is causing it. Can you help me?"

"That's a difficult one. I read recently that nine million Americans suffer from some form of dermatitis every year. You have to be a detective to find out the cause. It is usually by trial and error. It could be a food you are allergic to, the type of clothing you wear....Some people can't wear polyester—they have to wear cotton. Jewelry and cologne make some itch. Those who tend to be allergic have to use a hypoallergenic bath soap and detergent for washing clothes. Even nerves can make one break out in a bad rash. I know a woman who had a terrible rash that lasted over a year. She had trimmed her pyracantha bushes, had garden gloves on, but the thorns went through them and into the skin on her hands. Her doctor advised her to stop garden work and to wear gloves when washing dishes. Wish I could be of more help. Antihistamines may help. I do believe there is no cure for those, ah, who are so unfortunate to have this problem. Always, always give your clothes a double rinse in your washing machine and...and...keep lots of lotion on your dry skin—a special lotion."

"Thanks for the advice, Dr. Ben. Hope your callers haven't forgotten you. Good luck."

"I think my callers have forgotten me. I'd really like to hear from someone to know what's on their mind. Of course I assume there is a mind out there! Well, in the meantime I'll try to entertain you with something a friend of mine told me. He told me about this hawk who was in need of some female companionship. He left his nest and flew around as hawks do, and he found a dove. He took the dove back to his nest, and the dove settled down. She kept saying, 'I'm a dove, wanna make love? I'm a dove, wanna make love?' She just sat there and did nothing else. So-o-o, the hawk found himself unfulfilled and went out flying again and picked up a loon. He took the loon back to his nest, and the loon settled in and then said, 'I'm a loon, wanna spoon? I'm a loon, wanna spoon?' By this time the hawk was very upset and decided to make a third try. So he flew out to the lake at Washington Park and picked up a duck. The duck settled down, and the hawk said, 'Look, there's dove over there. All dove ever says is, "I'm a dove, wanna make love?" And the loon over there, all he says is, "I'm a loon, wanna spoon?" And the duck says—'" Dr. Ben gave a wicked little chuckle. "'You made a mistake. I'm a drake!'"

It was quite evident that there would be no callers, but it was almost time for the hour to end. Dr. Ben said, "This hasn't happened before. Sure hope the management will permit me to return tomorrow. Hey, we do have somebody on the line. Who's this?"

"This is Jake, and I want to tell you what a friend of mine said about you."

Laughing, almost whispering, Dr. Ben replied, "Perhaps I should be afraid to hear about it!"

"No, not at all. It's all good,"

"Okay, Jake, lay it on me."

"My friend told me you are one of the most brilliant and interesting people on the radio. He told me you are the essence of eloquence."

"Jake, you are too kind. I appreciate the compliment. Thank you."

"You're welcome, Dr. Ben. I haven't been listening to you for very long, but I've decided to turn your program on every day."

"Thanks again, Jake. Bye now."

It was time for Dr. Ben to close his program. He was in good spirits even if the morning had not been successful. There would undoubtedly be better days. He bid any listeners out there farewell and went home to take his dog for his daily walk. Maybe he would read Bobette's letters again after the walk. He had brought them home from the radio station.

In his mind he did wonder what Bobette looked like. *Yes, yes, one of these days I will meet her.* This thought went through his mind more than once. Were Dr. Ben and Bobette on the same wavelength?

Chapter 8

The Letter

Several months passed. Gloria had settled back into reality but still listened to Dr. Ben every day and was still under a spell at the sound of his delightful voice. It was evident that many other ladies adored him too. Gloria had the feeling that she was his number-one caller, or could it just be wishful thinking?

Some of the programs were mind-boggling. Dr. Ben had a way of making married women feel like they were missing out on the best things in life if they did not have an affair or two. Maybe that was only natural for him to have such an attitude. He was a young, swinging bachelor—at least that was the image he seemed to project. Strange as it seemed, the listening ladies in his audience agreed with him.

One day, though, he simply went too far with the subject. His quote from Oscar Wilde disgusted Gloria to no end: "The best way to get rid of temptation…is to yield to it."

She snapped off the radio. "I'll write him a letter—one that will open his eyes. It won't be full of compliments." She was furious. "What terrible advice!"

She wrote a long letter not full of the usual praise. She let him know she was not impressed by his smart statements and told him there were certainly more important things in life than sex, and one did not need to *get a little on the side* to have a satisfying marriage. She scolded him for encouraging young or even older women to yield to temptation. It was degrading to broadcast this nonsense on the air.

The letter didn't take too long to write even though she was full of rage. Gloria wasted no time in getting it mailed. Dr. Ben would receive it the following day. She did not sign it "From The Dr. Ben Admiration Society" as she had on many of her previous letters—just her radio name, Bobette.

When Dr. Ben received the letter the next day, he was amazed and somewhat amused by her outburst. He made it a point to mention her beautiful, feminine handwriting and the Libra wax seal on the back of the envelope to his faithful listeners. He revealed the contents. He confessed that the elegant stationery and perfumed message definitely turned him on. And again he encouraged those who felt the need to write to him, saying, "I welcome your letters." He did not apologize for any statements he had made.

Gloria still turned all the radios on every day and listened to his talk show. Several weeks had passed since she had called in to his program. Her hard heart was melting. That sly man still intrigued her. She wanted to forgive her idol for any misgivings she had about him. He spoke of the many foreign lands he'd visited and mentioned he had a college education when one of the listeners questioned his schooling and asked what jobs he'd had in his lifetime. "Many," was his reply.

Gloria was enthralled once again over the Man with the Magic Voice. Was he real? She hadn't kept track of just how many months she had listened to Dr. Ben. Her thoughts kept interrupting her dull routine of life. Why couldn't she think about anything else? It was perplexing. Gloria always checked her daily horoscope in the *Denver Post.* When she read that a Gemini may enter her life in the near future, it brightened her day, but the horoscope gave a warning as well: if you are married to an Aries, don't ever be unfaithful, because Aries never forgives or forgets. Richard was an Aries!

Today life seemed beautiful and was going along smoother than usual. Gloria had settled down to listen to the talk show. She had listened to Dr. Ben's presentation of the early morning news and decided, in general, that the news was rather depressing not only today but most every day. However, Dr. Ben's regular show was interesting, informative, and just amusing. There weren't as many medical questions asked as there had been in the beginning. People talked about so many different subjects. There was one lady named Greta who called now and then. She was amusing at times. Gloria had recorded some of her calls. She loved Greta's German accent but felt sorry for her hard life. Her husband had abandoned her and her three children. Dr. Ben was sympathetic and understanding. This was another one of his amazing qualities.

It was no secret that this communicastor with so much savoir faire and finesse had many faithful listeners. Almost every day they told him how much they enjoyed his program and his presentation of the early morning news. Dr. Ben even did a few of the commercials. Those were commercials worth listening to—so different from the ordinary kind. His descriptions were actually breathtaking. Was there anything Dr. Ben couldn't do?

Once, when his program was on in the late afternoon, he described the beautiful sunset. He described the blues, pinks, and hazy whites. He said, "Oyster pink or seashell pink." Gloria went outside to view the sunset. Another time when he was on a late-night show, he described the moon in such sensual, elegant adjectives that she actually stopped her ironing and went outside to behold this magnificent wonder. She never took the time to enjoy the beauties of nature, the majestic mountains, and so on. Life was busy and rush, rush, rush. Quite often Dr. Ben would say a few things in French or Latin. What a man. So unique…so unlike the other communicastors.

Dr. Ben's show was almost over. Gloria must have been thinking about other things. Then she heard something that gave her a sudden jolt. Had she heard what she thought she just heard? Dr. Ben made an announcement that he would no longer be on this station after this month. No reason was given.

Gloria thought, *It can't be. It just can't be! What will I do?* She was in tears by that time. Her day was ruined. She thought of Scarlett O'Hara and uttered in a low whisper, "I'll think about it tomorrow!"

Tomorrow arrived too soon. Gloria refused to believe her Prince Charming was going to disappear from her life. She convinced herself that meeting Dr. Ben was inevitable. She dressed in black—in mourning—because Dr. Ben was leaving…and black made her look slimmer. She looked exceptionally pretty and gave the illusion of not being heavy. She had lost some weight, as she was faithfully exercising.

Gloria had to take the bus to the radio station. It seemed to take forever to get there. But the big moment finally arrived: destination KXYZ. The lady in black nonchalantly asked to see Dr. Ben Carter. The receptionist said, "Just a moment. I'll see if he's here."

Dr. Ben walked into the front office. He was tall, had gray hair, and was not quite as young or handsome as Gloria had pictured in her mind. But his gaze was so penetrating, it made her quiver with joy. He motioned for her to sit down. There were a few chairs in the small but neat room.

Gloria looked directly into his sensual, brown eyes. "I'm Bobette. May I have your autograph?" She handed him a piece of perfumed stationery. Dr. Ben seemed a wee bit shy—not at all like the aggressive wolf-image he presented over the air.

He was still for a few moments, then wrote, "To a very dear and warm friend....From Dr. Ben and Major." Major was his dog, whom he loved and talked about so much on the air.

Dr. Ben and Bobette, as he called her, exchanged a few pleasantries and were completely fascinated with one another. Dr. Ben asked, "Would you like to have a tour of the station?"

"Yes, yes I would."

The tour was interesting and educational. Bobette had never been in a radio station. There were so many machines and gadgets. But more than the scenery, it was Dr. Ben!

Bobette certainly did not want to wear out her welcome or get him in trouble for neglecting his work. She said in a low voice, "I have to go now."

He walked her to the door and held her hand tightly in his. His searching eyes pierced hers. They were the bluest eyes he had ever seen. Their souls met as they stood so very close to one another.

Dr. Ben whispered into Bobette's ear, "Must you go?"

She departed in a hurry. Her imagination was scaring the hell out of her.

The next day she kept reliving the scene at KXYZ. It was so surreal. The fear still remained in her consciousness, but Gloria telephoned Dr. Ben after his program had concluded. They would not be on the air but on a different phone line.

"Hello, Dr. Ben speaking."

The sound of his voice made Gloria limp with ecstasy. She knew the gods were smiling on her because when Dr. Ben answered, he was truly happy to hear her voice.

"Ben, oh Ben, I am so sorry I left in such a big hurry yesterday. I...I...I turned bashful or something."

He didn't utter a word, so Gloria continued, "I've never felt this way before, and...and...I simply want to throw myself at your feet!"

Dr. Ben laughed in that alluring, adorable way. "Bobette, it's spring. That's what's wrong with you. You've got spring fever. That's what it is!"

They conversed for a few more moments. In a sexy, come-hither voice, Ben said, "Why don't you come to my apartment tomorrow for breakfast? I'll fix you an omelet. That will calm you down."

Gloria was absolutely speechless, and that didn't happen too often. She wondered if this conversation were real, or was she just having another daydream?

"Can you come tomorrow?" he murmured in an assured tone.

"Oh, oh Ben. I'd love to, but is isn't easy for me to get away. It would take some planning and maneuvering to do this. Ah…ah…let me think a minute. Sometimes I attend meetings, church, parent-teacher conferences, or astrology luncheons to learn about making horoscopes. I've got it! You could invite me to an astrology breakfast. That would certainly be a believable alibi."

They both agreed, but it wouldn't be for three weeks. Gloria had a husband who would not approve of her doing something two days in a row. Ben had out-of-town company coming; Gloria was busy with family activities. It was just impossible to get away on a minute's notice She would have to perform magic to keep this date on March twenty-fifth and would definitely have to be circumspect in each and every way. She pictured herself as a great general planning a strategic battle. Could she pull it off? Could she hack it? Time would tell. How would she react to the man of her dreams, to be able just to talk to him and not to have to hang up the phone because her time was up?

The days seemed to pass by slowly. In Gloria's eager anticipation and anxiety, she penned Ben a little perfumed note and sent it to his home address. It had all the glorification of her previous letters. It read:

My Dear Ben,

I am looking forward to seeing you. In fact I can hardly wait! I am delighted and frightened—in that order!

I am making myself a special dress for the occasion, and I hope you will like it. My family has gone snowmobiling today, so I won't be interrupted.

Please whisper into Mother Nature's ear with your sweet voice and tell her to make the weather nice for our day! Getting a car is out of the question. My daughter will probably be my chauffeur. I will have to be tricky. Pray for me!

Also, according to the planetary hours, 9:00 a.m. is an ideal hour for our meeting. Venus, the goddess of love, will be in full reign. I hope that is not too early.

Until then….

Love, Bobette

Chapter 9

Breakfast in Paradise

The days were passing slowly. Would March twenty-fifth ever appear on the calendar? There was plenty for Gloria to do, and she raced through her chores faster than usual.

It was depressing to have Richard on her case so much. At times he seemed more like her father than a husband. This was annoying to Gloria, but she didn't dwell on the fact. He always did his part and supported his family in style, but there never seemed to be a day when he didn't criticize her about something, even though she was a good mother, a good cook, and fairly good at keeping their house in order. She often wondered why Richard was this way but tried to overlook it because of his good qualities. A psychology book stated that criticism was the result of an inferiority complex. *Oh, this couldn't be the reason,* she thought. *Not Richard.* She put that idea out of her mind.

Gloria was in such a good mood, and nothing but nothing was going to spoil her state of euphoria. She had begun exercising and taking better care of herself in general. Brushing her long hair every night was getting to be a ritual. When she and Richard had been young and in love, he used to brush her hair. She had almost forgotten the good old days.

Richard did notice this change in his wife but didn't give it a whole lot of thought. However, when Gloria started painting her fingernails and toenails, he shouted, "What's going on with you? Who the hell are you trying to impress?"

"You, my darling."

There was dead silence after this response. Richard was no dummy and accused Gloria of lying through her teeth—and she was. He always thought she was lying when she told the absolute truth. This time he was right. She had lied. The grump was quite, and unequivocally, 100 percent right.

Gloria wanted to look dazzling for her breakfast appointment with Dr. Ben. She had a nice dress pattern she had purchased recently. It was a long dress with long sleeves and a low neckline. The material had been in her sewing closet for some time. It would be a snap to make. She had experience in this field; she had made lots of her children's school clothes and costumes for her daughters when they took dancing lessons. Gloria always sewed Easter dresses for her three daughters and herself and even made a pair of George Washington pants—jeans—for her son. Yes, and shirts too, bathrobes, and even kilts for Christmas gifts for the men in her family.

There was plenty of time for Gloria to get the dress made. Since the family left early in the morning, she could relax and delve into the sewing without interruptions. It took only two days in her free time to finish the dress. The material was so smooth and soft. The color was a beautiful delicate brown with a pattern of golden-tan flowers and leaves circulating throughout. The neckline was rather low.

If anybody had shoes, it was Gloria. Richard always growled at her, "You've got too many shoes for one woman!" Luckily there was a new pair in the closet, golden-brown suede with high tops and fairly high heels—so very sexy. They matched the colors in the new dress. The shoes were brand new and had not been worn yet. They were in style now.

Gloria even sang as she did her housework. She wanted to shout to the world that she had a date with the wonderful Dr. Ben Carter. She wanted to broadcast it to his listeners. How envious his female callers would be. They would just die!

The family could see how their mother's attitude had changed—even Richard. Not that he purposely neglected her in any way, but he did take her for granted.

Today was Saturday. Tomorrow would be the big day! The entire family—sons-in-law, grandkids, the whole tribe—was going snowmobiling. Although it was nice in the city, there was snow in the mountains. Richard urged his wife to join the group and told her she had been staying home way too much.

"Richard, I have to bake a cake to take to the astrology meeting tomorrow morning. Besides, I'm sick and tired of watching our grandkids. When I'm there, their parents think I am responsible for their welfare. They don't watch them! Besides, there's not enough snowmobiles to go around." Her answer made sense and satisfied him.

"Why in the world do you have to take a cake to the meeting?" he asked.

"I want to be different. The ladies will see my talent. Who knows? One of these days I may start my own bakery. I need the advertising!"

Richard just shook his head. "You have plenty to do right here at home."

The family said their good-byes to Gloria. Her favorite cookbook, Betty Crocker, was in easy reach. She found a good recipe for rich yellow cake—no cake mixes for this occasion! She divided the batter into three different bowls. Each layer would have a different color, blue, pink and yellow. All the food coloring was right there. This job was so enjoyable. Baking was one of Gloria's passions. Each color was mixed into the batter with care and love. Three individual pans were carefully filled and put into the oven to bake. The eight-inch layers baked perfectly.

After they cooled, they were ready to be iced. She would use creamy decorator's icing. How pretty the cake would be with different colored layers when it was cut. Gloria knew it would be pretty. She had done this many times for her children.

This work was so enjoyable. Icing the cake went fairly quickly. The decorating bags had been filled with different colors. Gloria worked with ease and anticipation, putting astrological symbols on the cake and the sun signs of the entire zodiac with their ruling planets. It looked good but not exquisite and elegant yet. Dainty little blue roses were made and put around the top of the cake. It looked professional—better than the picture in the cake decorating book! It certainly was to her advantage that she had a lot of cake decorating experience. When she took lessons, the class believed she was a pro. She did have almost a quarter of a century of practice, though, from doing cakes for her large family. That old cliché—practice makes perfect—was right.

At last Sunday, March twenty-fifth arrived. Why had it taken so long? Gloria was up bright and early—unusual for a sleepyhead. Richard was dressed and anxious to go golfing as usual. This morning, however, he did not rush off but kept his questioning eyes on his wife, watching her, gazing intently at her every move. She was trying to get ready for the astrology breakfast. Richard knew that Gloria was hung up on anything that pertained to astrology; he resented that she spent so much time reading about it. She had even taken lessons at Denver University. He had been horrified when she'd announced she thought there was something to reincarnation.

Gloria, still trying to get ready, put lotion all over her body. Richard still hovered over her.

"You never spend that much time getting ready for me," he said.

Wishing he would leave, Gloria began applying her makeup. He made her so nervous…as if she weren't that way already!

Richard growled and was very upset that Gloria was wearing her new dress for someone other than him.

"Richard, I asked you to take me somewhere last night, and you refused. Are you really jealous of a bunch of old ladies at an astrology meeting?"

He left without saying a word or kissing Gloria good-bye. She finished getting ready in peace. She had already inserted her diaphragm after her bath. Last of all, but not least, she applied her best cologne—Moon Drops—and donned her beautiful zodiac jewelry. This nervous lady took a glance in the mirror… and approved.

Gloria yelled at her daughter, "Come on, Jean, I don't want to be late! Why can't I borrow your car?"

"Mom, you know I have things to do. I have to have my car. What difference does it make as long as you get there?"

"It doesn't. Let's go."

It didn't take long to get to the astrology meeting.

"Mom, call me when you want me to pick you up. Around one, okay?"

Gloria refused her daughter's offer to help carry in the cake and the big astrology book. She waved good-bye to Jean.

The sun was shining. Mother Nature had listened to Ben. Gloria thought the apartment house was nice looking. He had told her he lived in apartment six.

"Six is my lucky number in astrology," she had told him.

Gloria went up the flight of stairs, her hands loaded, and almost tripped on her long dress. There was no apartment six, only one through four, so she went back down and went down a long corridor. There a large sign caught her eye. In big, red letters, it read: "MOTHER NATURE WAS HERE. COME RIGHT IN!"

How clever of Ben. How clever… and how terrifically romantic! Gloria knocked softly, almost dropping the cake and book. The door opened immediately, and there was Ben.

"Hello-o-o-o-o-o. Come in. What's this?"

She handed him the beautifully decorated cake. "It's for our breakfast, Ben. I had to make this meeting look authentic."

He put the cake on the table, which had a romantic setting for two. He gently helped her take off her coat.

"Well, here I am," Gloria said. "Robbing the cradle!"

He looked directly into her eyes. "Chronological age makes no difference."

Gloria's heart pounded; her stomach felt as if swarms of butterflies were having a Roman holiday in it. She thought she would surely melt right then.

She returned Ben's gaze. "How did you know I would come? You don't have a phone. I couldn't have called you if our plans had to be changed."

"I knew you would come. I just knew it."

They stood there, eyes meeting, souls touching. Suddenly it seemed as if they were old friends and not strangers. It was too quiet. The silence shattered the moment; they became tongue-tied. Gloria wanted to throw her arms around him, but she restrained herself. She was a lady indeed. She would have to be patient.

Ben began to get breakfast ready. He was organized.

"Ben, I won't help you," Gloria told him. "Frankly, I'm tired of being chained to the kitchen all the time."

He was busy at the stove. They made small chitchat. She marveled at his coolness and efficiency. She studied him and could not believe they were alone at last.

Ben was dressed very informally—a sweater, slacks, and Keds. Bobette—that was what Ben called her—felt so elegant in her form-fitting gown with the low neckline. It was not nearly as low as the pattern had suggested, but still low.

Bobette sat with her long legs crossed. Her ankles were covered also. Only her shoes peeked out. Her legs did not show one bit.

Bobette had written "Ben" on top of the cake when she had first gotten there. The icing had been a little hard in the tube and did not squeeze out the right way, and she was as nervous as a cat on a hot tin roof.

Breakfast was ready. They sat down to an amazing menu: omelets, English muffins, fruit ambrosia, tall glasses of fresh orange juice, and coffee. On the table were lighted candles. How magnificent! After breakfast, Ben and Bobette were too full to have cake. Ben and Bobette pushed themselves away from the table and walked slowly across the room to a small couch. They sat down close together. Major, Ben's big, black Labrador, came bounding over. He put his huge paws on Bobette's lap.

Ben scolded the dog and said, "I'll put him outside."

"He's all right. Let him stay. I love dogs." Bobette leaned down and began to pet Major's face. Major gave her big, wet kisses. "See, Ben? He likes me!"

Ben did not take the hint. He changed the subject by asking, "Do you like the pictures on my wall? Do you know what they are?"

Bobette squinted. "Are they seashells?" Then she got up and walked closer to the wall. One side of the wall was women's breasts, and the other side of the wall was women's derrieres. By that time she was blushing. *I should have known!* The thought had occurred to her that her Dr. Ben could be a pervert. She sat back down, crossed her arms, and hugged herself. The room was quite cool as the back door was open while breakfast was being cooked.

"Are you cold?" he asked.

Bobette looked directly into his brown eyes. "Yes!"

Ben's arms wrapped around her quickly, and his lips pressed firmly on hers. Bobette responded eagerly. At last she was in his arms. At last! Her heart pounded and felt as though it would break. She ran her trembling hands through his hair. "Ben, Ben!"

He put his hand on Bobette's breast and hugged her with his other arm, still kissing her. In a husky voice, he said, "Bobette, this couch is not big enough for both of us. Let's go to my bed."

He got up, shut the back door, locked it, and checked to see if the front door was still locked. He led her gently to the bedroom. Then he poured two glasses of pink Chablis in quaint ceramic glasses.

Bobette was transformed. Right now nothing mattered—only Ben. She was on cloud nine. Words were not necessary. He gently turned her around, unzipped her dress slowly, and began removing her clothing. He unrolled her nylon stockings so expertly and pulled them off very gently. He unfastened her dainty pink brassiere, and last pulled off her pink girdle and sheer matching panties.

Bobette apologized for the girdle. "I have to wear one."

Ben took a very long look at her. "You don't need one!"

Suddenly Bobette came to the realization that a complete stranger was staring at her nude body. She jumped onto the flowered sheets on the bed and pulled the covers over her, quite embarrassed. "I'm not putting on a floor show, you know!"

Ben took his sweet time undressing, and Bobette did not take her eyes off him for even a second. She was absolutely spellbound by the size of his already erect penis—and somewhat terrified.

"Hurry up," she ordered.

Ben crawled into bed. Instantly their arms found each other. Their lips and nude bodies blended into one. They were hungry for each other's kisses; the passion was overwhelming. Waiting for three weeks had seemed like an eternity for them.

Ben's breath reeked of cigarettes and liquor. Bobette did not mind it at all. She craved him and was pleased that he responded with such passion. He kissed her shoulders and sighed as he caressed her soft body.

"You smell so good," he said.

"It's Moon Drops." Bobette thought she was in heaven and closed her eyes. Her heart was pounding.

Ben felt it beating against his chest. "It's all right....It's all right." He continued with his love making.

"Ben, Ben, I'm in heaven. Do you hear the angels singing to us?"

"Yes, yes I do!" he whispered in her ear, kissing her again and again so passionately. His tongue found its way into Bobette's mouth. She groaned and returned his French kissing. In actuality she had never French kissed before, nor had she ever experienced such strong emotion and passion. Bobette's entire body vibrated. Ben was an artist at making love. He panted and shook with tremendous feeling. He kissed Bobette's firm breasts and massaged her everywhere. His hands were strong but oh so gentle.

"My Prince Charming, my sweet Prince Charming!" Bobette murmured into his ear. She caressed his body from head to toe. Every inch of him was loveable. When Ben was undressing earlier, she could not believe the size of his manhood—so huge. It sure did frighten her, but she was completely fascinated by the sight. Now, in bed, she dared to put her hand on it, rubbed it up and down, down and up. It was so hard; it felt delicious. Good, good! Bobette squeezed it and patted it.

"Lord, you've got enough to fill three women!"

Ben was definitely embarrassed and did not say a word but wiggled directly on top of her and inserted his glorious penis into her. Bobette was ready to consummate their love…or was it lust? The lubricating juices were already flowing. Ben proceeded very slowly, teasing Bobette. His large sex organ was just unbelievable—gigantic, thrilling. It was entirely inside, all the way into Bobette. Then Ben began pumping up and down with such force. Sweat poured from his brow. They stared into one another's eyes.

Ben gazed into the very depths of Bobette's soul. "Why the frown?"

"It must be my conscience scolding me. I am sorry."

In reality Bobette was remembering something her mother had told her: "It's all the same!" Her mother had been married three times.

Mother was wrong. Bobette hugged Ben all the tighter and wished this moment could last forever. He was the perfect lover. He was pumping up and down…hard…hard. The two of them became one; they heard bells ringing. The bed shook as they came to the grand climax. Ben's semen trickled everywhere.

Bobette loved the warm sensation and whispered coyly, "Don't get off me. Please don't get off!"

Ben closed his eyes and went to sleep on top of her, with his arms around her. He was totally exhausted.

In a while he awakened. He was receiving butterfly kisses from Bobette. She nuzzled closer to him and fluttered her long eyelashes against his smooth face. It tickled him; he squirmed.

"I'm giving you butterfly kisses, Ben."

He did not say a word. Bobette wished he would talk. His voice was an instant turn-on. She suggested he say something in French to her, which he obliged. Then there was no talking because his magnificent penis was erect again. Ben rolled on top of Bobette, and her pulsating vagina was ready for action. Words were unimportant now. They communicated via the windows of their souls—their eyes.

This second session of sex was just as beautiful as the first. What a man! Bobette loved the way she felt, young and beautiful. Well, forty-two wasn't old. She thought of the cliché "I think, therefore I am." Perhaps that was true. Wild thoughts were clouding her brain: *I might like to have Ben's baby!* Then Bobette came to her senses and remembered she had inserted her diaphragm.

The two lovebirds lay in bed with their arms around each other, basking in the morning's experience. The wine was still sitting on the headboard of Ben's bed. They picked up the two beautiful goblets, clinked them together, and made a toast: "To us!"

It was late. The hands of the clock had moved ahead too quickly. Time had passed like a whizzing bullet.

Ben put his hands on Bobette's shoulders. "I think it's time to put yourself together now."

She reluctantly took the suggestion, tore herself away from him, and redressed quickly. Bobette used the phone in an upstairs apartment—Ben's neighbor—to call Jean.

"You can pick me up at one o'clock. I'll be out front."

"Okay, Mom."

Ben and Bobette said their good-byes. Ben leaned very close. "Bobette, tell me your phone number. I never got it when you left it at the station."

"I'm afraid to let you have it!"

Ben said nothing. He certainly was not like his radio personality—lots of words, etc.

Bobette kissed him good-bye and forgot to thank him for the delectable breakfast and wonderful time. She was still on cloud nine.

She walked to the outside of the apartment house alone, carrying her purse and big astrology notebook. Jean was right on time. Bobette got into the little sports car.

"How was breakfast, Mom?"

"It was really good. The ladies all adored my cake, and…and I really learned some things about astrology that I didn't know."

Bobette had had a glorious morning and felt like doing a sun dance to the gods. They had been more than generous to her today. She hoped Richard had a fine time golfing and would go every Sunday now.

Chapter 10

Reflections of Yesterday

It was Monday morning. Had Gloria really attended an astrology meeting, or was it a dream? She wanted to shout to the world, especially to the KXYZ listeners, about the dreamy episode with Ben. Oh, the ladies would be so jealous, and one of the female communicastors would definitely be in that category. She might even be angry! She had a *thing* for Ben. All the women did. Gloria felt exceptional and quite special.

Was there life before coffee? Of course not! Gloria was back to herself now. It was still early morning. She had time to make coffee and have one cup before the daily schedule began. What a schedule, getting a husband and four offspring ready for work and school. Arranging bathroom time for each was a headache in itself. She did manage, though, and her friends admired her. She never seemed to receive any kind of admiration from the most important person in her life: her husband, Richard. They argued too much. It was an annoying habit. Jean had told Gloria, "Mom, Dad yanks your chain, and you react. He does it on purpose! Try not responding."

Gloria would change to a better mood when Ben came on the air at ten o'clock. It was true that she had never had an affair or even thought about one. As of yet it wasn't an affair, but maybe it had promise. Her existence had always been admirable. Overcoming evil had not been a problem. Yesterday did not seem evil. It had been pure heaven, and Gloria had never experienced such intensely passionate feelings in her entire life. It was frightening! Just thinking about yesterday made her quiver with joy. Maybe it had been just a one-time stand.

The day's newspaper was still on the table. The horoscope was waiting to be read. Gloria was a Libran. She knew exactly where the horoscope section was located. She read, "Libra: Behind that pretty facade is a smart, smoldering soul who knows how to get what she wants. When the scales find the partner they've been looking for, it could be a match made in hot heaven."

Ben was Gemini, the twins. It read, "Quick-witted and fun. Gemini will jump around from one lover to the next until they find the lover who is almost as smart as they are and able to keep up in a high-spirited race. Gemini is highly intellectual and won't hesitate to play mind games with a lover—it's mere child's play to them. The reward for those who can lasso a Gemini is a free-spirited lover who shines at parties but is a devil in the bedroom. Many Gemini are ambidextrous."

Gloria liked what she had just read. She had always placed a lot of faith in her horoscope; she read it again and again.

Dr. Ben was coming on the air now. "Good morning, my fine listeners. What's on our agenda today? Anything special on your mind, your...ah... gripes, your likes, dislikes? Call me, and get it off your chest. Have you noticed what a beautiful day it is? Oh.... Who do I have on the line now?"

"This is Adam, and...and...I want to discuss gossip."

"Okay, Adam."

"Do you like gossip, Ben?"

"Well...ah...well, yes, I guess I do. Doesn't everybody?"

All of a sudden the radio went off. No static—not a radio in the house was on. Gloria waited a little while, thinking it would be all right soon. She phoned her next-door neighbor. "Did you lose your power, Evelyn? Mine just went out."

"It sure did, and I'm not happy about it either!"

"Maybe it won't last long. I hate to miss my radio show. I'll talk to you later."

What a disappointment. Gloria had planned to call Ben on his show. Now she wouldn't be able to phone him even off the air. The whole radio station would be tied up. What a rotten development that was.

Ben wouldn't be on the radio too much longer anyway—just a week or two more. No reason had been given for his termination, and Gloria had completely forgotten to ask him about it. Maybe he was going on to bigger and better things. She thought about calling him later in the day when the power returned. She hoped he might still be there.

Several hours slipped by. Gloria dialed the office number at KXYZ. "May I speak to Dr. Ben Carter?"

"I'll see if he's here. May I tell him who's calling?"

"It's Bobette, one of his faithful listeners."

It seemed to take forever for Ben to answer. "Hello, Bobette."

"Hello, Ben. My power was out and I missed hearing you this morning. I just wanted to hear your divine voice."

Ben laughed a little bit. "And why is that?"

"I've become addicted to it…and to you."

"I like the sound of that. Do you want to give me your phone number now?"

"Yes, yes. Definitely yes." She gave him her phone number and said, "The best time to call is around 9:00 a.m., when I'm alone and can talk in private."

"Thank you, Bobette. I'll give you a call. Right now I have some pressing duties. Stay cool."

"You too."

The next day, at nine o'clock in the morning, the phone rang. Gloria hoped it would be Ben.

"Hello," she answered.

"Hello there. You said I could call at this time of day, that you'd be alone. When can we see one another?"

"Oh…ah…ooh…that's a good question. I'll have to think about it. Not that I haven't thought about it ever since last Sunday. Bless astrology! May I call you back sometime today at the station?"

"That's not really a good idea, Bobette. Some people around here have big ears. I'll call you when they are all busy, and we can talk freely—probably around one in the afternoon."

"Okay. Bye."

Gloria sat down to have another cup of coffee and to work on a crossword puzzle. As a rule there was never time to do that. Today was different. But how could she work on a puzzle and figure out how to sneak away for a few hours with Ben? Impossible! She did not have a car.

Ben kept his word. The phone rang promptly at one.

"Hello," Gloria answered.

"Why hello there, Bobette. Any…ah…ideas.?"

"Well, nothing original. I could meet you at the church that is just a couple blocks away from my house….And then…then—"

"Yes, and then you hop into my car, and we can go to a motel. I'll rent a room for tomorrow. I'll be at the church at noon. How does that sound to you?" Ben said in his tantalizing, come-hither voice.

"Sounds like a plan! Hey…why can't we go to your place?"

"The painters are there, painting the entire apartment building. Probably be there for two or three days. Too many people, and the paint fumes might get into my apartment. Besides, we need privacy."

"Until tomorrow, then." Gloria sighed and blew Ben a kiss through the phone.

"Yes." Ben blew a kiss back.

Gloria didn't know how she could get through the day; it seemed to go so slowly. Just anticipating the next day was making her behave like a teenager with a big crush—not on an older man but on a younger man. Ben was ten years her junior. As he had said at their first tête-à-tête, chronological age made no difference!

Gloria spent the rest of the day on mechanical, repetitious tasks: doing laundry, getting a meatloaf ready for dinner, and baking a cherry pie. As a rule the family looked forward to dessert. The kids took turns clearing the table, washing the dishes, drying them, and putting them away. Sometimes they needed a little help with homework. Richard or Gloria was always available for them.

Later that evening, Randy was complaining that he didn't have his project ready for school, and it was due the following day.

Gloria asked him, "Randy, why did you wait until the last minute?"

"Mom, I have to practice for basketball. Remember? I'm on two teams!"

"Okay. I will help you. We can do a poster…of a zodiac wheel…with all the astrological signs on it."

"Gee, Mom, that sounds like a good project. Do we have any poster paper?"

"Luckily we do have some in the basement—in the junk room.

Gloria and Randy got the materials together: colored pencils, pens, glitter, and anything that might be useful.

"Mom, here's some little stars, the stick-on kind," said Randy.

First they needed to make a perfectly round circle for the zodiac wheel, but no protractor would be that large. Randy found a large cardboard circle in Gloria's airbrush articles and asked, "Will this work?" He drew around the edge of the circle with a pencil.

"Perfect," said Gloria. "Get the yardstick. We'll need it to make twelve equal spaces from the center of the circle. Here, look at my picture of the zodiac and you will know what to do. It is only black and white. This one we are making will have colors."

Randy did as his mother instructed. "Wow, Mom, it does look like a zodiac wheel."

"You print so well Randy, so number each space starting here—one through twelve."

"What is that for?

"Those are the numbers of the houses. There are twelve houses in the zodiac. Each one represents something. Number one is yourself, personality, and physical appearance. Number two is the money house. Three is communications, siblings, and lower education. Four is home and ma and pa figures. Five is love affairs and children. Six is employment, health, and pets. Seven is marriage and partnerships. Eight is death, rebirth, and reincarnation. Nine is higher education, religion, philosophy, and journeys. Ten is social status, ambitions, and career. Eleven is friendship, and twelve is undoing. Each house has its zodiac sign beginning with Aries, then Taurus, Gemini, Cancer, Leo, Virgo, Libra, Scorpio, Sagittarius, Capricorn, Aquarius, and Pisces."

"I can't remember all that, Mom."

"I can, so start with number one. Use pencil, then we'll go over it with colored pencils and colored gel pens."

"This looks like it will be a real winner. Maybe I'll get an A in this psychology class."

"Randy, better count on an A+ because this work is going to be fantastic!"

Gloria and Randy worked for two hours or so. Randy had the printing in exactly the right houses on the zodiac wheel. Gloria told him what color to use on each house. It was turning out better than she had imagined. When it was completely finished, she put glitter and stick-on stars here and there.

Looking at Randy, Gloria said, "Be sure to bring this poster back after it's graded. We'll frame it and hang it up in our rec room downstairs."

The evening had gone by very quickly. It was relaxing to have her mind on something constructive, but suddenly it went back to Ben. *What in the world am I doing? What am I thinking—another rendezvous with Ben? I'm out of my mind! Should I cancel the date for tomorrow?*

Chapter 11

Extracurricular Activity

Another day in the adventures of Gloria. Things seemed to be going quite smoothly, and breakfast was cooked just right. The family ate in shifts. Richard was the first to leave and then Randy, who gave his mother a good-bye kiss and thanked her again for all the help she had given him on his poster.

He carried the large zodiac poster ever so carefully because it was truly a work of art, and he was proud of it. He had his own car; the other kids took the school bus or rode with friends. The youngest, David, walked to the elementary school as it was very close.

When Randy went out the door, his mother said, "Now, don't forget to bring our poster back after your teacher grades it because I want to hang it up somewhere downstairs."

She watched Randy as he walked to his car, and she thought, *He's such a handsome boy. Well, in reality, all of my kids are so good-looking!*

The other children left on schedule. The two youngest always watched *Underdog* on TV. It came on early, so it didn't interfere with their schedule. It was a good cartoon. After the family had left for the day, it was so quiet and relaxing. But quiet time did seem to fly by. Occasionally Gloria would invite her neighbor over for coffee or vice versa. They were good friends.

Today was going to be a special day. Gloria would take special pains to make herself beautiful. She was very sure she could steal away for a couple of hours without anyone knowing. On the other hand, she could be pressing her luck! She would chance it. She felt as if lady luck were on her side.

Gloria had a radio in almost every room of the house, even in the bathroom and the basement. She would listen to Dr. Ben's program while she was getting ready for their wonderful date. "I will have my bath first," she said.

Gloria leisurely pampered herself in a lavender-scent bubble bath. When finished, she felt rejuvenated. She was not paying full attention to Dr. Ben's program as she brushed her long hair. Suddenly Dr. Ben's voice came through: "Yes, we can talk about the deaths of prominent people. One was Onassis. No one has mentioned him today except for one person. I happen to know that Aristotle Onassis was born in Turkey. Well, it's now part of Turkey, and he had rather humble beginnings as a tobacco merchant. I'm not sure it's necessary to talk about his death, but he was a prominent person."

Gloria was trying to listen to Dr. Ben but couldn't help anticipating their meeting in a few hours. She polished her fingernails and toenails and was thinking of what to wear. Maybe casual dress and running shoes. High heels would not be appropriate to walk the two blocks to the church where they were supposed to meet. Gloria donned her dainty pink panties and bra first, then pink capris, a delicate, off the shoulder pink blouse, white tennis socks with a little pink flower design, and new sports shoes.

She stood in front of the little radio beside the tall mirror in the bedroom and glanced at herself. Ben's voice came through—that wonderful voice. He was still talking about Onassis.

"When Turkish troops captured his hometown in 1922, he fled to Greece and then to Argentina."

Ben laughed a little. "What is it about Argentina that gets so many people going? Aristotle Onassis began working as a telephone operator and a lineman for the Buenos Aires Telephone Company in 1923 and worked his way into the tobacco import business. In 1930 he was named Greek consulate for Argentina. That was only seven years after he began working as the telephone lineman. The next year he entered the shipping business. He took advantage of a wave of currency evaluations that allowed him to buy three freighters at a bargain price of a hundred and twenty thousand dollars. He went on to build one of the largest privately owned shipping fleets in history. He was a millionaire by age twenty-five. He conducted a long affair with Maria Callas. In 1968 he married Jacqueline Kennedy. Oh my goodness, I'm out of time. I've been rambling on. Time to go. My name is Ben Carter, and I'll talk to you again tomorrow morning on KXYZ. Drive carefully, and be gentle with one another."

Gloria's mind was not on Aristotle Onassis at the moment because it was almost time for her to meet Ben. She went outside and picked a pretty pink rose. Ah, the roses were so beautiful in the yard. Gloria went back in, looked in the mirror, and put the rose in her hair and fastened it with a bobby pin that had a sparkling jewel on it. *Mmm, I look pretty good. Wonder what Ben will think?* She put some items—a surprise for her lover—in a big, black, beaded bag, locked the front door, and walked quickly to Grace Community Church.

Ben's car, a white Ford, was there—the only car in the parking lot. He opened the door for Gloria. What a gentleman!

"Hello, Bobette."

"Hello, Ben."

"What've you got in your bag?"

"A little surprise for you, but you have to wait."

"Okay."

It didn't take long to get to the motel. There was a sign in front—the Dusty Rose Motel—and there were all shades of red and pink roses in the surrounding flowerbeds. It was a beautiful sight. Ben led Bobette—she was strictly Bobette now—to the room he had previously registered. It was number six. What a good omen! Six was Bobette's lucky number.

The room was very clean, quite small but acceptable. Ben closed the blinds. Bobette strode into the bathroom with the large handbag, saying, "I'll just be a few moments." She quickly undressed, hung up her clothes on a hook, and took out Ben's surprise: a black push-up bra, crotchless black panties, long, black fishnet stockings, and black high-heel pumps. Bobette wasted no time in getting into the outfit. She finished with a few drops of her favorite cologne, Moon Drops, and then pranced slowly toward Ben, whose eyes were wide open with surprise and admiration.

He uttered, "Ooh...la la!"

Bobette leaned on him. "I'm going to undress you." She unbuttoned his shirt so slowly, deliberately taunting him, then unbuttoned the top button of his slacks and pulled the zipper down in slow motion. She gave him a gentle push onto the bed. "Lift up your feet so I can take your pants off."

"I have to take my shoes and socks off first."

"Let me do it, honey chile."

Bobette was being too slow. Ben's anticipation was almost too much. Off went the pants, and Bobette literally ripped his boxers off as his manhood was already popping up.

"You little vixen," Ben muttered breathlessly. "It's my turn now to undress you!" He sat up on the edge of the bed, and Bobette proceeded to sit down on his lap. It was inviting—in her mind, delicious. Ben unfastened her bra so tenderly and gently. *He must have had a lot of practice* was the thought running through her head. Then Ben lifted Bobette up and laid her on the bed, pulling her high heels off and carefully removing her long, black fishnet stockings. Bobette was quivering as Ben kissed her stomach while removing her sexy, crotchless panties.

"Okay. I can't wait one minute longer," Ben whispered in her ear. He flipped the covers down, put his strong arms around Bobette, and began kissing her on the lips, ears, neck, shoulders, and absolutely everywhere on her entire body.

"Oh, my Prince Charming, ooh." Bobette returned his kisses with a passion she had never known existed. "Ben, Ben….Ooh…oh….You make me feel so alive."

He said nothing but continued the thrilling lovemaking. Words were not necessary.

She fluttered her long eyelashes against his cheek. "Do you know what I'm doing? I'm giving you butterfly kisses."

Ben muttered, "Um…ah, okay."

"Ben, Ben…do you like me?

"I like you *too much*!"

He rolled on top of her, and she sighed. "Take me. I'm all yours."

He did take her, easily at first, teasingly slow, and then he whispered in her ear, "Do you want me?"

"Yes, yes, yes I do want you!" She wanted and desired Ben like she had never wanted a man before. What was this strange but magnetic stranger's hold on her? Was it fate?

They made wild, passionate love, and it was wonderful—a new and a different world. Exhausted, they lay in each other's arms until it was getting late and time for Bobette to get back home to her normal life. They got dressed and opened the drapes in room number six.

"When can I see you again, Bobette?"

"I can't say right now. I'll definitely keep in touch, though."

They hugged. Bobette kissed Ben on the lips. Their meeting had been wonderful today but did not have the exquisite ambiance of their first encounter. There would be more pink Chablis, soft lights, and music next time.

Ben and Bobette said good-bye to the Dusty Rose Motel. He drove her back to the church. As she was getting out of his car, she started to cry.

"What's the matter?" he asked.

"Oh, oh Ben. I forgot to put my diaphragm in! Oh God, I could get pregnant. What'll I do, what'll I do?

Ben said, "Come closer." He put an arm around her. "Don't fret. I've had a vasectomy!"

Chapter 12

All Good Things Must Come to an End

Gloria thought of herself as Bobette now because she had felt beautiful and full of life ever since meeting and getting to know Ben. She was still basking in the previous day's adventure with him. Today the sun was shining, the grass was green, the flowers were in bloom, and Bobette had spring fever. Ben had changed her life. She'd had no guilty feelings whatsoever about her indiscreet actions over the past few weeks. She wondered why not.

Bobette wanted to shout to the world that she was having the best time of her life—an affair with the great Dr. Ben. Wouldn't his female listeners be jealous? Of course, Bobette was still in fantasyland. She came back down to earth and remembered the fact that she had a great husband and five wonderful children. Many blessings were hers. Had she gone stir-crazy mad? In all the years of Bobette's married life, she had always been true blue and entirely faithful, until Ben. As far as she knew, Richard had always been faithful to her.

Why oh why did Ben have to leave the radio station? Bobette would have been content to just listen to her beloved every day and get goose pimples all over at the sound of his voice and laugh. Perhaps the devil had taken hold of her! It was a sad day when Ben was no longer with KXYZ, a sad day indeed. There was no rhyme or reason to why the management had let him go, and Bobette wondered why she had never asked him.

Ben and Bobette's romance continued for seven months. They would meet at his apartment, sometimes at a nice out-of-the-way motel, and yes, even at Bobette's house occasionally. It was a miracle they never got caught. It was too good to be true.

One time, in Ben's arms, Bobette confessed to him, "Ben, Ben....You... you make me feel like a teenager in love. Something else too—I want to touch you like I've never touched a man before!"

Ben was silent but continued the lovemaking. He must have been delighted with the compliment she had bestowed on him.

Bobette, at times, would whisper to him, "Make love to me. Make love to me 'til I die!"

Ben would respond with a chuckle, "That would be a long time."

"But what a way to die!"

Checking the Gemini and Libra horoscopes was a daily routine. One day for Gemini Ben, it read, "Gemini is the master of seduction, trying anything and everything anywhere." That was so right. One time Ben and Bobette made passionate love under a blanket in the park and other times in the car in a secluded place.

Bobette's horoscope for Libra read, "Libras make very imaginative and creative lovers, willing to try something new, a passionate fire that cannot be extinguished." Another time she suggested to Ben that they have sex on the giant beanbag in her living room. "Pretend you're going to rape me," she teased. Ben did as she directed, and oh, how interesting it was.

Bobette was always sending Ben a note, letter, or picture of something she had drawn. One time she sketched a cute donkey and printed in fancy letters around it, "Good ass is hard to find!" Ben did enjoy the cards and letters she sent him. But come to think of it, Ben had never written a letter or sent a card to Bobette. Perhaps she was the aggressor. She would have been delighted to receive anything from him.

She was completely delighted when she'd drop by his apartment and he was in his usual attire—a terrycloth kilt with absolutely nothing underneath it. He was so different, so completely different from any man she'd known, but he was the *best*! He knew a lot about a great many different subjects. Bobette told him he was a walking encyclopedia. Ben would only laugh and not comment on it.

At the moment Bobette's favorite song was "Me and Mrs. Jones." She'd often hum and sing, "Me and Mrs. Jones, we've got a thing going on....We both know it's wrong."

One sad day, though, Bobette's euphoria came to a crashing halt. She called Ben. It was her usual routine. In a very stern voice, he said, "It's over!"

"No, no," Bobette cried. She couldn't believe what she had heard. "Why?"

"Don't call or write anymore!"

"Never?"

"Never!"

"Never is a long time," Bobette sobbed.

"It's over. Take this from an old, seasoned veteran." He hung up rudely.

After a few days, Gloria called the radio station. *Maybe the station manager can give me some insight*, she thought.

"Did you keep all the letters written to Ben from his admirers?" she asked the manager, Mr. Babcock.

"Oh no. He probably put them under his pillow and slept on them."

Gloria and Mr. Babcock talked for some time. He stressed that Ben had an inferiority complex.

"Thank you so much for your time, Mr. Babcock," Gloria finally said. "I appreciate it. I sure do miss Dr. Ben's radio show. Good-bye."

Sometime earlier she had asked Ben what jobs he had held in his life. Ben had rattled off quite a few. "I've been a radio news announcer, a disc jockey, a radio talk-show host, a nurse, a social worker, an author, and a speaker; and I even have a couple of degrees."

Later, Gloria/Bobette, in her mind, was wondering why Ben was just a talk-show radio communicastor when he had so many credentials.

Another day, in one of Ben and Bobette's conversations after their lovemaking session, Ben had confessed to Bobette that he had an ex-wife and four children. That had blown Bobette's mind. She had thought he was a young man who had never been married! Ben was not close to his children. Ding ding....Why hadn't that rung a bell? He did have many friends who, perhaps, were his family. One very good friend had co-authored a book Ben had written about Colorado history. There was just no end to Ben's capabilities. Strange thing, though: he did see a psychiatrist every now and then. It had been mind-shattering to Bobette when that bit of information had been revealed to her by Ben himself.

Gloria did not need a "shrink." That was what Ben called Dr. Brahms. Gloria had not a soul to confess her experiences to. She had no degrees or college education, but considered herself very common-sense smart. Never; in her entire life, had she been rejected. This was a bitter pill to swallow! She simply could not accept it.

Wallowing in self-pity was not Gloria's style. But she was so depressed and crying on the inside, she decided to make an appointment with Ben's shrink. She had to talk to somebody or go crazy. She did check out Dr. Brahms's credentials and found he was one of the best.

Dr. Brahms's office was located in a respectable neighborhood. Gloria had no trouble driving there. The red-brick building was surrounded by tall trees that gave shade, and there were pretty flowers in the front. It did look more like a home than an office. Gloria opened the front door. There was nobody there. She figured she was in the wrong place. In five minutes a young man appeared in jeans and sandals with his toes hanging out, no socks.

"I'm Dr. Brahms, and you must be Gloria," he said as he took her hand.

It took a moment for Gloria to realize this young upstart was the psychiatrist. How could it be? She had expected an elderly gentleman with gray hair and spectacles.

After this shock Gloria poured out her story to the doctor from the beginning to the end. He was not sympathetic and told her to go home and make her marriage come alive! His last words rang in Gloria's ears: "Ben Carter just might not be the man you think he is."

Gloria/Bobette was reflecting on one of her past experiences with Ben. She had told him that she had a dental appointment on one specific Monday. The dental office was right next to a 7-Eleven store.

Ben had said, "Would you want me to meet you there at eight-thirty a.m.?

"I'd love it," Bobette had replied.

The dental appointment hadn't taken long—no cavities, and the hygienist cleaned Bobette's teeth quickly. Things were running smoothly. Bobette glanced in the mirror before leaving and smiled at herself. "Nice job." She hurried down the flight of steps and walked briskly to the 7-Eleven. What luck! There was Ben's car waiting for her. Bobette excitedly opened the passenger door.

"Boy, you timed that just right!" What a complete shock! It was not Ben at all, but a very good-looking young man.

"Oh, I'm so embarrassed," said Bobette. "I thought you were someone else. I'm so sorry!"

He leaned forward. "It's all right. Get in!"

The car looked exactly like Ben's. Bobette ran to her own car and drove straight home. She was full of anger and not admiration for Ben. When she talked to him, he did not have a valid excuse—or any excuse. Bobette, still too naive, did not see the light. Stubborn as a mule, she refused to come to the conclusion that the good times were over. But why? They had such wonderful chemistry.

Two weeks after the appointment with the shrink, she broke down and, against her better judgment, called Ben. He did not have his own phone, but his neighbor who lived upstairs, Karen, was kind enough to let him use hers now and then. Bobette dialed her number.

"Hello," Karen answered.

"Hello, may I please speak to Ben just for a minute?"

"I'll see if he's home."

When Ben heard Bobette's voice, he became totally unglued and did not give her a chance to say a word. "We've had some good times," he said. Then he shouted, "It's over! Don't call me anymore. Don't bother Karen with your phone calls, and don't write me any more letters!"

It was about time that Bobette got the message loud and clear, and the years to come would prove just what kind of man Ben Carter really was.

Chapter 13

Memories

Bobette's/Gloria's ego had come to a crashing halt. How could such a sizzling relationship come to such a disastrous end so soon and in such an ugly manner?

Why, she had always been her daddy's darling and her momma's angel, never had anyone hated her; as far as her memory served. But Ben seemed to hate her, and did say he never wanted to see her again. Any respectable person would have said this face to face. He was not respectable. Ben was a fickle Gemini according to her astrology books. He did have fluctuating moods that were puzzling to her.

What irony. Gloria had time on her hands now because Richard was into golfing lately and was gone more than usual. But...but....her lover was gone... gone for good. Gloria thought *What did I do that was so wrong? Was I just too aggressive? Why didn't I play hard to get?*

It was hard for Gloria to act like a happy little housewife when she was so desperately depressed—like the old song she was "Laughing on the Outside (Crying on the Inside)."

All Gloria did when she was alone was think about Ben and the wonderful times they had had. It was unbelievable that in all of her life, her heart had never been broken. It wasn't only broken now, it was *destroyed*! She wasn't like Scarlett O'Hara saying, "I'll think about it tomorrow." She wanted to die. She had never felt this way in her entire life.

The memories were so haunting. One instance stood out in Gloria's mind. She and Ben had been in bed in a motel room, having their little tête-à-tête after the love making, which was always great. She had brought a tiny can of baby powder and rubbed it all over his body, which he had thoroughly enjoyed. "Wow, I've not had that kind of a rubdown since I was a baby," he had said.

Ben had seemed somewhat tired and wasn't his usual charming self. Bobette had asked him, "Why are you so mean to me?"

"Because I'm a bastard!" he'd replied.

Bobette had been astonished. For once she had no response. As a rule words just flowed out of her mouth. Richard always told her, "You talk too much!"

Gloria thought perhaps she should see Dr. Brahms one more time. He hadn't charged her the first time she was there. Maybe luck would be on her side once more. Gloria called, and the secretary said, "You'll have to wait a week. No openings until September sixth at eleven-thirty a.m."

The days passed slowly. Finally September sixth arrived. The waiting seemed like an eternity for impatient Gloria.

Dr. Brahms still looked like a baby to her with his sandals and the unprofessional style that accompanied his attire. He didn't give Gloria much chance to say what was on her mind.

"I can't believe you haven't done a thing I've told you," he said. "This double life you're leading is not acceptable. Did you ever stop to think that Ben could blackmail you? The trouble with you is you want to have your cake and eat it too!"

Dr. Brahms was not interested in anything Gloria had to say and told her to get professional help from somebody else.

"I don't need professional help," she replied.

"Gloria, I wish you could be tested. I do believe you have a high IQ. I think you could write short stories. Put a lot of sex in them."

"Thank you, Dr. Brahms. I'll try."

Gloria had asked Dr. Brahms the date of his birthday. He was a Pisces. The astrology book read, "You can tell a Pisces, but you can't tell him anything."

Every day after the suggestion, Gloria made notes for a future story. She had a difficult time believing that Ben, the wonderful, benevolent man whom all worshipped, could be so cruel to her when they had such a history. Gloria had thought she knew him well. She didn't know him at all. On the air Ben had been described as one of the most brilliant, most eloquent, and most interesting people of all time.

Astrology still played an important part in Gloria's life. She would read her books often. The thought of reincarnation had never entered her mind, but the books implied that one has many lives. Gloria's family thought she was crazy to believe this nonsense. Fortune telling also was one of her interests. As a little girl, her mother would go to a fortune teller now and then, taking Gloria with her. Fortune telling was against the law, so it was disguised as a luncheon. The ambiance was inviting: a dark room, a candle glowing, a few pieces of food. The fortune teller was always in costume.

"My goodness gracious, I think I'll go to a fortune teller." Gloria made an appointment that very day even though the price was a bit high.

Gloria rang the doorbell thinking a lady in dark clothes and fishnet stockings would appear. No, just an ordinary housewife. No dark curtains and glowing lamp, certainly not the days of old. Oh well. They exchanged pleasantries and then got down to business. They sat down at a kitchen table, and there was no crystal ball or Tarot cards.

The fortune teller said, "Give me your hand."

Gloria held out her left hand, palm up. "Oh, a palm reader."

The reading began. "You are so uptight and have lived many lives…not been back long." The palmist looked at Gloria's hand intently. "God, you're romantic! Easily bored, but a good mother. You've worked hard."

Gloria's hands were rough; that wouldn't have been hard to figure out.

"You have four children," the fortune teller continued.

"No, five."

"I see a big change as there is a break in your lifeline. Two marriages. Your son will go to college. You have many talents." The palmist seemed to be legitimate. "Gemini will be in your life. He keeps you young. Yes, yes, definitely call him. God brought him to you."

It seemed the reading was over much too soon. Gloria was shown to the door. Maybe the palm reader was better than the shrink. Maybe. Time would tell.

Next time I see a fortune teller, Gloria thought, *I hope to have it as it was when I went with my mother. That was the ultimate experience. This was almost boring.*

Bad memories crowded her mind. There was the time she had questioned Ben: "If my circumstances change, will that make a difference?"

Ben did not say a word.

"Tell me, why can't you say?"

"That's my position. I don't have to reveal it!"

"May I keep writing you letters?"

"Ask Dr. Brahms. You know I give your letters to him."

"Oh Ben, he does me more harm than good."

"Do you like my letters?"

"I find them amusing—mildly amusing."

That was a turn off. Mildly amusing—when she poured out her heart and soul? Not too long ago, Gloria and Richard had a terrible argument. Richard always got upset on little trifles that didn't amount to a hill of beans. His face had turned red and ugly even though he was so handsome.

He had blurted out, "I can't take it anymore. You're a fucking bitch!"

Those words had hurt so much. Gloria had grabbed her purse and run out the door, started the car, and driven off madly. "I don't know where I'm going, but I'm going." She stopped at a payphone booth by a Piggly Wiggly grocery store. She called Ben at the radio station. He didn't answer; she got only the answering machine. Her message was loud: "Ben, I'm having a bad, bad day. I'm not going home. Wish you'd talk to me. I don't know what I'm going to do."

She stood there for a few minutes looking in her purse. Yes, yes, the answer was there: her free winning coupon from a country-music station for a one-night stay at an elegant hotel. Gloria won prizes frequently from radio stations; she was smart or just plain lucky.

"That's where I'll go!" She checked in at the Brown Palace. It was so plush. A basket of fruit adorned the desk. She helped herself to an apple and some grapes. It didn't take any time to settle in. All Gloria had was her purse and a small amount of money.

The first thing she did was to call Ben again. He may as well spend the night with her. But he did not return her call. Richard was not worried about her absence; the kids thought she was staying with a relative. No big fuss was made about her absence.

A few days later, when Gloria finally talked to Ben, he gave no reason or excuse for not joining her at the hotel. And this was the man of her dreams!

After thinking over the whole episode, Gloria remembered something she had read recently: "the hottest love has the coldest end," by Socrates, a Greek philosopher. He definitely hit the nail right on the head.

Chapter 14

Life Goes On

Life would simply not be the same. Gloria had no idea how to cope. Should she take the psychiatrist's advice to make her marriage come alive again? Could that be possible? Maybe possible, but not probable. She tried to remember all the positive things in her marriage. There were many. There were more in the years Gloria and Richard had been dating. They had, in all reality, been together for the biggest part of their childhood. They had been eleven years old when they had first laid eyes on one another. Gloria had gone outside of her apartment house to empty the trash. Richard was outside and started throwing snowballs at her. Gloria saw his face. He was kind of cute. He had on a hooded gray sweat jacket. She didn't notice the two other boys who were with him.

That day she emptied the trash several other times…just because. To make a long story short, they went steady most of the time until they were nineteen; then they got married. They were childhood sweethearts. They did not have the beautiful wedding that most girls dream of. They walked to the church. Gloria's father and stepmother walked with them. The church was Trinity Methodist; the minister was Samuel Dawson. The flowers looked real although they were artificial. There was a photographer there. The pictures turned out excellent. Gloria was always so sorry not to have had the beautiful wedding she deserved. She secretly thought Richard's mother would have had it annulled. She said they were too young to get married and it wouldn't last more than three months anyway. She had been wrong.

Gloria listed all of Richard's good qualities and all of Ben's. Richard was far ahead. He was much better looking, he was a great cook, he was a natural-born mechanic, and he could fix anything. Ben was educated but had to call a repairman when something needed fixing. Both were good in the bedroom. There should have been no problem in the decision.

Gloria couldn't seem to get her life back to normal and wrote a letter to her favorite astrology magazine, thinking any advice would be helpful. The letter read:

> I was born on September 24, 1927, at 6:30 a.m. MST. My husband was born on April 9, 1927, at 6:30 a.m. MST. We love one another, and although we disagree on everything in general, our life has been good in most respects. We have five children. For several months I listened to a young man on the radio. One day he announced he would no longer be with the station. I had fallen in love with his voice, so I made a special trip to the station just to meet him, as I had talked on the phone with him many times. I was delighted when he invited me to his apartment a few weeks later. We had an affair—a short one. He has now rejected me. He has psychological problems. His former wife left him, as did two other women. I have this uncontrollable obsession to be with him. He acts as though he hates me. He was born on May 28, 1937 time unknown. I consulted a psychiatrist. He said this man is not what I think he is and to concentrate on improving my marital relationship.

It took forever and a day for her letter to be answered. The horoscope magazine sent a letter back telling her it would be a few months before it would be published in their magazine.

Gloria had almost forgotten about the letter she had written about advice on Ben's total rejection of her. Family life had gone on as usual, and things were good.

One day the long-awaited magazine was stuffed in the mailbox with the other mail. When it was noticed, Gloria tossed the other mail aside and went straight to the advice column. "Now maybe I'll get some answers!" she said.

It had the letter she had written, printed and edited. The title was "EMOTIONAL CAPTIVITY." It showed the zodiac wheels of Libra, Aries, and Gemini with their horoscopes and the placements of the planets at Gloria, Richard, and Ben's dates of birth. How fortunate. It would have cost a lot of money to have that done. This was what the astrologer wrote:

> Your letter has been edited. You are a Libran with the sun placed in your third house of communications, ideas, and short trips. It is in conjunction with a fourth-house Mars in Libra and in company with the moon and Venus in Virgo. Libra as a sign is incurably romantic, and often the daily monotony of a humdrum existence is more than these natives can bear. With your sun opposed to ninth-house Uranus in Aries and also in out-of-sign opposition to late Jupiter retrograde in Pisces, you are a taker of chances on the emotional level. Your time of birth gives you the moon-ruled Cancer rising, so you are sensitive to others' opinions, but your Venus in Virgo, falling in your third house in square to Saturn in your fifth house of love affairs in Sagittarius, indicates you are chronically emotionally discontented. Venus square Saturn always wants what it can't have. Saturn rules your sixth house of marriage, Capricorn, and afflictions to this planet do indicate that your unions are not as happy as could be.
>
> The man born on May 28, 1937, is a Gemini native. He has his birth Mars in Libra on your sun-Mars, a potential physical tie but one carrying a great deal of stress. Your Virgo Venus is exactly opposed to his Saturn in Pisces—a very difficult aspect for emotional happiness between two people. As his Saturn is square his own sun, and his sun is square his birth Neptune in Virgo as well as your Venus, he is a very unstable person when it comes to emotional fidelity. Your obsession with him can be denoted by your Virgo Venus conjunct his Neptune, an aspect of fascination that may indeed border on

> illnesses. His former experiences with women should cause you to run as fast as you can in the opposite direction.
>
> During your involvement with him, your progressed moon in Gemini had come to his birth sun, so you were fascinated by his speech or his native mercurial talents. Your husband has an Aries sun and moon in Leo so has better contacts with your chart. His Taurus ascendant and Venus in Taurus rising, in trine to your Virgo moon, is quite a stabilizing force in your life. Perhaps the Taurean placidity is too tame a vibration for you to consider exciting, but you would do well to make an effort for renewal.
>
> Transiting Saturn now in Cancer, adverse to your Mars in Libra, may cause you to sever a relationship with him that you would probably regret. Saturn's contact with Pluto in both your charts within the next year may instigate deep discontent in each of you; however, this will pass over in just a short time. With Jupiter now transiting Pisces and currently in your eighth house, a better physical relationship with your husband should be initiated. Your Gemini friend is not the man for you or, indeed, for anyone. Do not allow transiting Neptune in Sagittarius square your Venus in Virgo blind you to the real consequences of your obsession. Don't confess to your husband; Aries is a notorious example of never forgiving a mistake. Make a new start.

The advice made sense—same thing Dr. Brahms had tried to tell her. Astrology certainly had its merits. It hit the nail right on the head, so to speak.

Writing a book would not be an easy task. Should Gloria take the advice of Dr. Brahms and write short stories? He did say he thought she had a talent for writing. She would rather author a novel—romance of course! There were notes in her desk about talk radio that could possibly be a start. One documented a call she had made to Ben in his early days on KXYZ:

"Hello," Ben had answered in his charming voice.

"Ben, I forgot to ask you something."

"Yes?"

"Do you know what *loquaciousness* means?" the caller asked, thinking this word would stump him.

"It means 'talkative.'"

"Astrology says Geminis are loquacious. Well, you aren't when it comes to me."

"So much for astrology," he smugly replied.

"What do you think about chain letters?"

"They're against the law, and frankly it's a waste of time."

Gloria had received a chain letter now and then and always replied. Ben was right because nothing ever came of them; someone broke the chain and didn't follow through.

"One more thing, Ben. Did you read the article 'Does a Secret Relationship Enrich Your Life' in the Sunday paper?"

"Yes. I did."

"I think I could write a better one," Gloria bragged.

There was no response. Ben's silence was exasperating!

Gloria realized there was no use in reliving the good times with Ben. It was over. She could still hear him screaming at her on the phone, "It's over! It's over! Take it from an old, seasoned Veteran. Quick surgery is the best!" He had not let Gloria get a word in edgewise on that fateful day.

Dr. Brahms had told Gloria she was a masochist. He was wrong. Inflicting cruelty on herself was not her cup of tea. Maybe he was implying that she inflicted cruelty on herself by associating with Ben when he was so wishy-washy. Now maybe, just maybe, Ben was a sadist—he loved women and then dumped them if they got too serious.

Gloria sighed. "And to think I was so proud that Ben let me in his life and swept me off my feet. I felt so honored to be in his presence! What a stupid fool I've been. How can I go back to my humdrum life?" Surely there had to be an answer.

It would have been a positive thing if Gloria would just count all her blessings and take time to stop and smell the roses. She would never seek counseling. She was smart enough to figure out an answer to her situation. Gloria realized she had one precious advantage in her secret affair: she never got caught, and that was a true blessing in disguise!

Would this experience make her or break her? Only time would reveal the outcome. She couldn't sleep at night; she was a total wreck. Dr. Brahms had the nerve to tell her to slit her wrists! What kind of a doctor could he have been?

This affair had been purely something easy, trivial, and insignificant for Ben. For Gloria it had been overwhelming and mind-boggling. It seemed akin to death.

Chapter 15

Another Radio Personality

Gloria decided to put her best foot forward and get back to her normal life. It wouldn't be easy. Was anything in life easy? Maybe for those who were fortunate to be born with silver spoons in their mouths! Those who had the world at their feet and were still not satisfied went on to alcohol and drugs; some even died from overdoses.

Gloria started out her new regimen by cleaning the house thoroughly. The basement was just full of stuff, but it was good stuff. Richard had bought nice big, white cupboards for cooking utensils, the Tupperware, his paint and supplies. One room, which was supposed to be an exercise room, had a treadmill and other equipment to keep one slim but was completely filled up with way too many boxes. It was a disgrace. Gloria's mother had passed away some time ago. Since Gloria was an only child, she had inherited everything of her mother's. It was simply too much.

Richard and Gloria had a garage sale. It was such a large amount of work. The day was beautiful; a lot of people came. They only were interested in guns, jewelry, and camping equipment. That was a waste of time. People weren't interested in beautiful dishes, knickknacks, clothes, curtains, etc.

Exercise was on the new agenda also. Jack LaLanne was on TV every day. He made exercising seem like a joyful thing to do. Most of the time Jack had his big dog on with him. Jack LaLanne advocated eating the right food and living life in a productive style. Sometimes Gloria's daughter would join her in exercising and was so happy that her mother had become involved and excited.

The two of them had a good time exercising to Jack LaLanne and listening to him talk about his dog. The exercising was a thrill instead of a drag.

Time passed. Talk radio held no interest anymore for Gloria. The other DJs and communicastors did not compare to Ben. A country-music station caught her fancy. The songs were all the "do me wrong" ones. Well, she could certainly relate to some of the sad songs. There was one DJ who seemed somewhat entertaining. His voice was fairly nice, although not like Ben's. There was nobody that could even begin to compare to Dr. Ben. Gloria had no clue as to why she put so much emphasis on one's voice. She felt listening to music was helpful when household chores were being done. Love songs were inspirational, but sad ones were not. What was that old saying? "Music soothes the savage soul." That was something to be experienced.

Forgetting Ben was an impossibility. Gloria had tried several times to get in touch with him but to no avail. Being a Gemini, Ben was restless and fickle. His dual personality worked overtime. It was loud and clear that he had washed his hands of Bobette.

Months and months slipped by, and there was no word from Ben. Was he all right? Did he have a job? Heaven knew Gloria had enough to do to keep her thoughts occupied. But it did not work. Her hands were calloused and rough from working in the huge yard. Her youngest child said, "Mom, your face looks young, but your hands look old!" That was a low blow, but kids tell the truth.

It was quite time-consuming to take care of the big house and huge yard. David loved to drive their tractor mower, so it was not a problem to keep the grass mowed. Richard supervised the mowing and did the edging. There were many Juniper and Pyracanthas in the front yard. Definitely it was the most beautiful yard in the entire neighborhood. Richard spent a lot of time trimming the bushes to perfection. He took great care of the rose bushes and one very large Alice Dupont Mandevilla plant. It was a climbing plant. The neighbors always commented on how gorgeous it was. It was a long name to remember.

Gloria's mind was taking control of her thoughts. She had almost wished herself dead when Ben had dumped her. She just could not forget the months they had spent together when Ben was so attracted to her. Gloria wished she hadn't come on so strong. She shouldn't have let him know how much she cared. She adored Ben. It must have frightened him away! He had said to her that he did not want a jealous husband gunning for him.

All the women loved Ben, so why should he waste his time on a female who would bring him nothing but misery and trouble? Gloria did not understand her wild obsession with him and how she had let her obligations fly out the window. She knew she was a bright, intelligent being. The psychiatrist had led her to believe so and instructed her to make her marriage come alive with Richard. An astrologer had told her to occupy her mind with more intellectual pursuits and to try meditation. He reminded her that her progressed moon in Gemini, Ben's sign, accounted for her strange behavior. Gloria could hear his last words: "If you can succeed in keeping your emotional head above water, your feelings will pass, and the light of understanding will erase their shadows." Ah, beautiful words…but just words.

The country-music station did not replace the talk radio at all, but it would have to suffice. Jeremy was the morning DJ. Gloria turned her little radio on, and there he was talking.

"Are there any requests today?" he asked. "Just call me."

Gloria thought she may as well call him and request a song. "Hello, Jeremy. I'd like to request a song, please."

"I have a young lady on the line who wants to make a request. What song do you want to hear?"

"I'd like to request 'I'll Always Love You.'"

"Okay, young lady, and to whom would you like to dedicate it?"

"I'd like to dedicate it to Ben."

"Here it is—'I'll Always Love You" dedicated to Ben…from a *young lady*!"

Gloria was somewhat amused by the "young lady" emphasis. Jeremy had no idea of the age of his caller. Her voice did sound much younger than her chronological age, many of her friends had told her. It was a fact.

After a month or so, there was a contest on the country-music station, KLZ FM. When the mystery song was played, the tenth caller would win a CD of George Strait singing old country favorites. Gloria liked contests and had often won prizes on another radio station that played big-band music. Somehow it seemed to be losing its popularity with the younger crowd.

Gloria felt lucky. When she heard the mystery song being played, she dialed the number several times; she was beginning to lose hope of even getting through. Then, amazingly, the line was ringing and not giving a busy signal!

"Hello, who is this?" Jeremy answered.

"This is Gloria. I hope I am the tenth caller."

"Gloria, you are the tenth caller. You are my lucky winner today! Congratulations."

"Thank you, thank you. I love KLZ FM!"

"Stay on the line for a few minutes. I need some information while we're off the air. You'll have to come pick up your prize. We've stopped mailing them—cutting back you know. Is that all right?"

"I guess so….Might be a while before I can make it."

Jeremy laughed. "That's okay. You have thirty days' leeway. The station is open from nine a.m. 'til five p.m. on weekdays. Hey, I'll get to meet ya!"

Jeremy's enthusiasm did not impress Gloria one iota. She listened to his country-music radio station out of pure boredom.

The very next day, Gloria called Jeremy again. "I'd like to dedicate a song."

"All right, caller. To whom would you like to dedicate the song? What song do you want?"

"'Come Live with Me.' It's for Ben from Bobette." Gloria was secretly hoping Ben would be listening and maybe call her.

Jeremy asked Gloria, "Who is Ben anyway?"

She gave Jeremy a brief description of her love affair with Ben; he interrupted while she was still talking. "To hell with Ben! What about us?"

Gloria was quite taken aback and practically shouted, "I don't want to become involved with anyone ever again, especially a Gemini. You did confess to me that you are a Gemini, which definitely means you are unpredictable and impossible. You can be hot one minute and cold the next. My astrology information tells me Gemini is the butterfly of the zodiac."

Jeremy was speechless for once.

Gloria still called Jeremy every day to make her dedications to Ben, but this DJ was so entertaining and very witty. He made her laugh when she insisted on being sad and plain depressed.

"Self-pity is for the weak. It's time to throw away your crying towel," Jeremy ordered her on one of the phone calls. "No more songs for Ben, okay?"

"Okay, Jeremy. By the way I will see you tomorrow. I plan on coming by the station to pick up my free CD."

"Be looking forward to it, young lady."

"I am not young! I am twenty-two years older than you."

"You sound young to me, honey."

"Compliments will get you everywhere. Just kidding! Don't get carried away now. I really am one hundred years old."

"Well, darling, my cock is really eight inches long, and I'm not kidding, You're going to love it!"

"Dream on, young'n. Good-bye now."

Jeremy had often discussed life and his conquests with Gloria. What a braggart he was. Nothing he said was impressive, simply amusing.

The next day arrived. The sun was shining brilliantly. Richard had agreed to drive Gloria to the radio station to get her free prize. He grumbled, "I'd just as soon buy you the CD and save money on the gas it takes to drive out there."

"Oh Richard, don't be so conservative and negative all the time. It's your day off from work, so relax and enjoy the scenery along the way."

It didn't take very long to get there. It did seem to be out in the sticks—kind of like the country. It was a good thing Richard was driving. He always knew exactly how to get anywhere and seldom got lost. The radio station was very small and not impressive; it looked just like an old house, not a business. Large, leafy trees surrounded it, shading it entirely.

Impatiently Richard growled, "I'll wait in the car. Hurry up, and don't take all day!"

Gloria said nothing but wished Richard wouldn't be so grouchy. He was completely cantankerous. She got out of the car and walked up to the front door. A sign on the door read, "Welcome." Gloria walked slowly in. There stood Jeremy, the young communicastor and DJ. Yes, he also broadcast the news. Gloria didn't listen to Jeremy giving the news, just the songs he played. She was not addicted to him. Jeremy had flaming red hair and a mustache. He was quite thin.

"May I help you?" were the first words out of his mouth.

"Yes. I came by to pick up my free CD I won a couple weeks ago."

"What's your name?"

"Gloria Madsen."

"Gloria, Gloria. Just a minute. Jeremy was staring a hole through her. He fumbled through the files and found her CD. He handed it to her, along with his name and home phone number. Then both of his hands were all over her. He was trying to feel her breasts. What an introduction—just unbelievable.

"Don't get carried away, Jeremy. My husband is right outside in the car. He told me to hurry up." He was still trying to grope her. "Let me go…now, you, you octopus!"

Gloria hightailed it to the car.

"Took you long enough," said Richard.

"I'm sorry."

"What was the problem?"

"Oh, the jerk couldn't find my name in the CD file. He wasn't too swift."

Richard accepted the explanation.

What a surprising experience. Jeremy was so forward and had a cocky personality. Such nerve he had. He did not even know Gloria, but his hands were all over the top of her body. He was like a giant octopus. His name should have been Mr. Octopus!

Little did Gloria realize how this meeting with the young upstart would eventually evolve. Right now she was mortified and just wanted Richard to drive away from there. She wondered why she even bothered to listen to the radio in the first place.

Chapter 16

Disparaging Situations

Several weeks passed. Gloria had listened to the country-music station but had not called Jeremy. He was still entertaining and nice to hear on the radio. Out of sheer boredom, she picked up the phone and called him at his home. She figured he would be there.

"Hello."

"Hello, Jeremy."

"Gloria, it's you! Where've you been?"

"Right here at home, just getting over the shock of your octopus arms."

"Well, toots, are you ready to come visit me at my apartment and get laid?"

"Not sure yet," Gloria teasingly replied.

They talked for five minutes more and decided Friday morning would be a good time.

"Call me on Friday," Jeremy whispered, trying to be coy.

It was two days until Friday. "I think I'll be maternal and take Jeremy some cupcakes I baked myself," said Gloria. "I'll do some for my kids, of course, because I will do clown cupcakes." Gloria was adept in the baking department. She loved decorating cakes and fun cupcakes. Her mother-in-law had told her she should open a bakery because her cookies were so good.

Gloria put on her apron and got busy. It was still early in the day. She had plenty of time. She made one and a half dozen cupcakes called half and halfs. They were half chocolate and half white. The icing was white, and Gloria piped on colorful clowns. She had learned that in a cake-decorating class some time ago. Every now and then she managed to take some kind of a class at one of the nearby schools.

Friday finally arrived. Gloria telephoned Jeremy to let him know she would be there. His phone rang and rang. He didn't answer. He must still have been asleep. He was a sleepyhead.

Gloria had on one of her nice, casual slacks suits. She chose the blue one to match the color of her eyes. The cupcakes were neatly arranged in a pretty white box with a ribbon tied around it and a big blue bow. She hoped Jeremy would be impressed.

No car today; she had to walk a block to the bus stop and wait twenty minutes for the bus. It finally came. The driver was very cordial. "Good morning, ma'am."

"Good morning," Gloria replied. "Will you tell me when we get to Bannock Street? That's where I need to get off."

"I'll be glad to. Have a nice day."

"Thank you. You too."

The scenery along the route was interesting—lots of apartment houses and big, green maple trees.

"Bannock Street," the bus driver yelled. Gloria pulled the cord for the buzzer. The bus came to a stop. Gloria held her purse and cupcakes carefully as she stepped down the three narrow steps.

It wasn't too far to Jeremy's address. He had given expert directions. His apartment number was not six, her lucky number.

Gloria knocked on the door at number ten. By that time she was wondering if she were doing the right thing. She knocked and knocked. Nobody came to the door. What happened? Then she called a cab, thinking the bus was out of the question. The mood she was in now was pure anger. She wanted to get away.

The cab driver arrived in a very short time. His driving was that of an expert; he had his passenger home in double time. Gloria paid him the fare and, as a tip, gave him the cupcakes.

When Gloria finally got Jeremy on the phone, she was livid. "Jeremy, where were you? I spent hours preparing for our rendezvous, lowered myself to take the bus, even made and decorated cupcakes for you. Just where were you?"

Jeremy was not talkative but answered, "I told you to phone first."

"I did, but I thought you were asleep." She yelled, "Well, where were you?"

"I had a better offer!"

"How do you know it was better?" Crying, she went on, "What kind of a creep are you? Are you trying to destroy me?"

Jeremy was truly shocked by her violent outrage and began to speak very slowly. "Well...well...you're not my mother." Long pause. "And you're not my wife."

"But I am a *human being*. You said you were going to screw me. If you wanted to back out, why didn't you just say so?" By that time Gloria was screaming. She just couldn't believe this situation.

Jeremy meekly said, "Well, I just wanted to screw up your mind."

Gloria was hysterical and yelled, "Well, you sure did a good job of it, you little son of a bitch." She slammed the phone down so hard, it was a wonder that it didn't break right in two.

It was still early in the day. Gloria was considerably shaken. She looked at the calendar hanging on the kitchen wall. For heaven's sake. It was Friday the thirteenth. No wonder it had been an awful day. Maybe there was something to superstition after all, even if she didn't believe it.

What didn't kill Gloria will make her stronger! That happened to be one of her beliefs. Another thought: *idleness is the devil's workshop.* Who had time to be idle with a husband and four offspring and a big house to clean? Gloria did believe that pain and boredom were the foes of happiness. She was not happy today because her anticipation had been shattered. In truth she was acting like a frustrated teenager. Many times Richard would say to her, "Oh grow up!" Gloria didn't want to—her second childhood was much better than her first.

Wallowing in self-pity was not the thing to do. Gloria decided to cook an extra special dinner with the clown cupcakes for dessert. The family was delighted with her broiled chicken, mashed potatoes, corn on the cob, Texas toast, and milk. The cupcakes topped it off.

Richard asked her, "Whom are you trying to impress?"

"Just trying to make points with you. They say the way to a man's heart is through his stomach."

It seemed to work. The family was in a good mood.

Three weeks later Gloria phoned Jeremy at the radio station and requested the song "How Do You Mend a Broken Heart?" Evidently Jeremy didn't put their conversation on the air—he had pushed a button.

He asked, "How do you mend a broken heart? Chew bubble gum, honey, or else take a razor and slit your throat!" With that sarcastic statement, he hung up on her.

Three weeks passed. Not a radio in the house was on. The phone rang.

"Hello," Gloria answered.

"Gloria, this is Jeremy."

"What do you want? You're on my blacklist."

"Please forgive me. Just listen."

"I'm listening. Make it quick."

"I want to pick you up after my doctor appointment tomorrow. Then we'll go to my apartment."

Gloria agreed. The next day couldn't arrive fast enough. Jeremy said he would call before picking her up. Once again she got dolled up to perfection. The phone rang at exactly 11:00 a.m.

Gloria, almost singing, said, "Hell-l-l-o."

"I'm not coming." It was Jeremy.

"Not coming! Why?"

"I'm sick. I have the flu, and my nose is running.'

"Jeremy, darling, I'll make you feel better. I really will. Please come," Gloria begged.

He replied, "Damn it. I can't make love when I'm sick! Besides, I'm tired, and I'm going to crash right now. Good-bye."

Chapter 17

Shocked, Chagrined, and Surprised

As the expression goes, third time is a charm! Gloria did not count on it. Jeremy was not like any person she had known—charming sometimes and despicable other times. And Gloria hadn't forgotten about Ben. He had always been a gentleman with perfect manners and never used bad language. What a difference between the two Geminis, even though they both had brown eyes and were born in the South!

Nothing excited Gloria these days—not family vacations, trips to Disneyland, or company. Ben had opened the door to heaven and then sent her to hell. Jeremy did say he would make Gloria forget about Ben; that he would be like filet mignon after Ben, who was hamburger. What a braggart!

Jeremy invited Gloria to his apartment two weeks later. It would be early because he had an early class. He was going to college part-time.

This particular day started out as usual with getting the family off to work and school. Gloria did not loll around having coffee. She ran her bath water and put bath oil on so her skin would be silky smooth. She did not forget to insert her diaphragm. Gloria shaved her long, slender legs and lay in the blue tub for a few moments, letting the bubbly water caress her body, while she anticipated the meeting with the young DJ. He was only twenty-four years old. Gloria forgot how old she was. Jeremy was so frisky! He made Gloria feel young.

Gloria's curly hair looked fantastic. She put on her makeup with the skill of an artist. Her reflection in the full-length mirror showed an elegant image: a beautiful lady in a two-tone, metallic orange dress and silver high heels. The silver Libra zodiac necklace and earrings completed the outfit.

Gloria was able to borrow her daughter's sports car and it did not take long to get to Jeremy's place. The traffic flowed quickly. Gloria wondered if the young upstart would even be there. It was true he had stood her up twice. Yes…yes...he was there! His blue Volkswagen was parked right there in the parking lot. Gloria hurried up the steps of the old but impressive building and opened the front door to the apartment house. There, coming down the stairs, was the fantastic Jeremy with a wastebasket in his hands, barefoot and wearing a pair of tight cutoffs and no shirt. His legs were quite good-looking.

"Hello," he said. "I'll be right back as soon as I empty this trash."

Gloria ascended the stairs as though she were in a dream. She did think it was only a dream. Apartment ten—there it was. She went inside. It was very neat and tidy—not at all what she had expected. Things were so in order. His bed was made; it had a panda bear on it. Gloria was impressed—her maternal instinct. There were shelves and shelves of books. Was he a well-read young man? Large maps covered the living-room wall. A guitar, a stereo, and a recorder were in view, and not a dirty dish in sight. A large bell hung in the doorway between the bedroom and living room, supported by a blue velvet ribbon.

Jeremy was back in a flash. "Sit down. I'll get you some coffee."

Gloria sat down in a leather rocking chair and put her feet up on the ottoman. She was handed a heavy mug of coffee. Jeremy got himself coffee and sat down, not next to her but clear across the room.

"Cream and sugar?" he asked.

"No, I'm sweet enough," Gloria purred.

They chitchatted a bit, then Gloria took something out of her purse. "Here's the record I wanted you to hear."

Jeremy took it and put it on his stereo record player. The music started out slowly and dreamily: "Gloria, Gloria."

"Yes, I've heard it before…just forgot it."

The phone rang. It was one of Jeremy's friends needing to talk and needing a shoulder to cry on. Jeremy was in no hurry to hang up.

Gloria sipped her coffee and thought, *My God, he's just like Ben—a regular do-gooder, solving everybody's problems!*

At last the telephone conversation ended. Maybe it wasn't so long, but it seemed like an eternity to Gloria.

Jeremy lit a cigarette. There was a knock on the door, and without hesitation a visitor came bouncing in as if she belonged there. She was a very attractive gal in a mini skirt. Jeremy and whomever she was started talking and completely ignored Gloria. Finally Gloria spoke up as Jeremy did not have the courtesy to introduce the two.

"You must work at the radio station too?" Gloria asked.

"This is Barbara. She's the secretary," Jeremy casually replied.

The conversation between Barbara and Jeremy went on and on. They talked about the radio station and how she was not getting a fair shake. Boohoo!

By that time Gloria was about ready to throw up. Instead of getting violent or making a scene, she just walked slowly out the door; the two were in such deep conversation, neither noticed her leaving. She ran down the stairs, jumped into her daughter's sports car, and peeled down the street.

Gloria muttered to herself, "I can't believe what happened. Jeremy is simply incorrigible. If he and that bimbo had a ménage à trois in mind, it won't happen with me! I should've stayed—at least made a scene or done something besides run away like a wounded animal."

Gloria slowed down, knowing it was unsafe to drive recklessly, and thought this situation could have been a coincidence—maybe but not probably. At that moment she hated the intruder, hated Jeremy, and even hated herself. The beautiful day had turned into a nightmare. One thing was certain: Gloria was not going to play second fiddle and wait in line for Jeremy's favors. No tears were shed even though the hurt was devastating.

Instead of driving home, fate seemed to take a hand, and the sports car reversed its direction. It seemed as though the steering wheel guided Gloria straight to Ben's apartment. She rang the doorbell and was trembling, thinking he probably wouldn't be there anyway—not during working hours.

Gloria/Bobette hadn't seen Ben in over a year. He had threatened to call the police if she ever darkened his doorstep again. She rang the doorbell harder, almost in a panic. Her body felt as if it could explode. Words rang in her head: "You little fool! Don't you know you're treading in dangerous water?" She again knocked loudly on the door.

It opened very slowly. There stood Ben looking all bedraggled.

Bobette hugged him tightly. "Ben, Ben, I thought I'd never see you again. Dr. Brahms said you were dead to me!"

"You've caught me in a very weak moment…a very *weak moment*!"

"Good God, you look terrible!" Bobette walked in. The room was so dark. "I'll open the drapes."

"No!"

Ben's room was a total mess; he'd been painting. The two of them sat down on his couch, and Ben started crying. Bobette sympathized and put a tender hand on his knee.

"Don't," he said.

"What is the matter?"

"I'm in love with a married lady!"

Bobette put her arms around him and hugged him tightly. Their cheeks were touching.

"I haven't shaved," Ben said.

It had been a long, long time since Bobette had seen him. She looked directly into his eyes. This scene did not seem real. The two of them sat there just not saying anything.

It's all right." Bobette ran her fingers through his hair and gently caressed his whisker-covered cheeks. The next minute the two of them were on his bed.

Still crying somewhat, Ben confessed, "I have my needs." He was not crying as hard now. Bobette hugged him tighter; he responded somewhat, then he got out of bed. "I've got to be alone for a while." Ben walked into his living room completely nude and then returned after a few minutes.

All this time Tchaikovsky was playing loudly on the stereo. In the midst of their lovemaking Ben shook his fist and just sobbed; then he said, "Stop. Listen to that passage."

Bobette sobbed too. "I'm nothing but a slave, a servant." Their tormented souls embraced; their nude bodies molded into one as they floated on a cloud of misery and pure ecstasy.

Ben held Bobette tighter and sighed. "Stay…stay for two days."

Bobette wanted him to say, "Stay forever." She must not have been thinking clearly. What about her husband and children? The fact that Ben wanted her so desperately was frightening. He had never said these words before. Bobette wanted to stay forever; however, that dream was not possible at that point in time.

Bobette did not ask Ben about the married lady he was in love with. It seemed not to matter to either of them in their moments of pure lust. After their intense sexual encounter, they started some casual conversation. Ben asked Bobette how her belly dancing was progressing.

"How did you know I was taking belly dancing?" she asked.

"I read your letters."

"Dr. Brahms said you did not read them."

"I read every one of them."

Bobette responded, "This is fate. It was meant to happen."

Ben turned on his record player. Bobette grabbed a wrinkled pillowcase to use as a veil and began to sway as she whispered, "I'll seduce you."

"No."

"Let me try."

Bobette remembered some of the belly dance steps and then did the inch-worm on the floor. It did impress Ben, who was intently gazing at her moves. He had put on some red boxers before the dance.

The dance was over. The music had stopped. Bobette went over to Ben and yanked his boxers down. "Oh, what pretty, bright-red boxers you have."

"I'm not that way."

Bobette was not sure what he meant by that, but knew that sex was on his mind.

The couple made their way to the bed again.

Ben groaned, "Oh, you feel so good."

He and Bobette made wild love again and embraced one another with savage hugs.

"Oh, did I hurt you?" Ben breathed in Bobette's ear.

"No, no. It feels so good." Bobette was crying. She loved him so much.

"I want complete abandonment now. Relax."

Ben gave Bobette the ultimate kiss: cunnilingus—a brand-new experience for her.

What would the future hold?

Chapter 18

Time Marches On

Life was unbelievable. Gloria's once-mundane existence had been full of excitement and thrills. Maybe she should write a book—pure fiction. Nobody would believe her wild double life, and it just might be a best seller. There she went daydreaming again.

Jeremy was out of Gloria's life now, and Ben, who had purposefully rejected her. How many times had she heard the statement "it's over"? For the time being, it would have been sensible to get on with her life. Actually, her life was better than most. Richard took care of her and the children. He was a great father, but he did have a way of making Gloria feel quite insignificant. However, she did not have an inferiority complex. In fact she thought quite highly of herself. Didn't psychology books say you have to love yourself? Richard told her she was a follower, not a leader; little did he know. If she ever wrote her story, it would blow his mind, but then he didn't like to read, so no worry.

Gloria decided to settle down, attend to her wifely and motherly duties, and try to forget her indiscretions. She had always been a wonderful mother. She would try to take the advice that had been given to her: to make her marriage come alive again. Was this possible? Not a snowball's chance in hell! But, as they say, miracles do happen.

Life went on with family activities, camping, waterskiing, snowmobiling, company from out of town, and a funeral now and then. That was enough to keep a person busy.

Gloria often wondered if God would forgive her. She forgave herself. If Richard hadn't golfed so much and left her out of his life completely, she may not have strayed. However, this was debatable. Richard still had a domineering, rude way of putting Gloria down, of making her feel like a second-class citizen, a lowlife. Could it be he was the one who had an inferiority complex? Interesting! He was an Aries, so that didn't seem feasible. Aries are the leaders of the zodiac.

Years and years flew by. The kids had grown up. Gloria took several classes at a community school. She had many interests, but didn't seem to learn enough, or follow through. Gloria was a jack of all trades, but a master of none.

Time went on. Gloria did not listen to the radio talk shows anymore. They were dull. There were plenty of family activities to keep her occupied. She often wondered if a broken heart were more painful than real pain. Of course it was—no need to ponder that thought. Bette Davis said, "Pleasure of love lasts but a moment. Pain of love lasts a lifetime." Gloria thought perhaps she could find some love quotes by famous people and put them together in a notebook. Maybe this was pure nonsense; maybe not. Maybe she should write a book on the subject of rejection; she had experience in that department. The smartest thing to do would be to forget the past, but how could she forget all the wonderful (and some not so wonderful) moments with Ben?

Gloria remembered something that had happened one time when Ben had partially rejected her. It wasn't all negative. It was a day when Gloria had worked hard and felt as if she could use a little relaxation, a change. Thinking of Ben revived her. She took a bath, applied some makeup, and ran a brush through her thick, curly hair. Casual clothes would have to do. Gloria's memory served her well. She relived the experience in her thoughts and even remembered the words she spoke to her daughter.

"I'm going to the library. Be back in a while."

Her daughter was doing homework and didn't bother to notice her mother's departure.

The sun had just set, and twilight was descending upon the earth. Gloria arrived at Ben's in twenty minutes. By that time she had become a reliable driver. A few months earlier, she wouldn't have dared to drive more than twenty miles an hour. Tonight she zoomed along at forty-five miles an hour. Practice does make perfect! Gloria easily turned into the driveway of the apartment house.

Ben's light was not on. His apartment was dark. Gloria knocked on the door, rang the doorbell, and knocked again louder. "Darn." The word formed on her lips. Instead of leaving she walked to the back of the apartment building. It was difficult finding the right apartment. Aha—there was a cute little patio. It had to be Ben's, and the sliding door was open a whole six inches, but the screen was locked. Ben had to be home. His drapes were closed.

Gloria/Bobette walked to the front of the building and opened the door. Just a few steps to the apartment. She knocked gently but got no answer. She turned the doorknob. Wonder of wonders, it was unlocked, so in tippy-toed Bobette; the persistent female.

A small candle burned in the living room; eerie shadows flickered on the wallpapered walls. Bobette walked to the bedroom thinking Ben must not be there. Yes, yes, yes, he was there, fast asleep with a heavy blanket over him; it was pulled up right under his chin.

The room was so cool. Ben must have been a fresh-air freak!

Bobette just sat on the bed, looking at Ben and admiring him. She leaned over and kissed him gently on his mouth.

Ben opened his eyes very wide, closed them, opened them again, and shook his head in complete disbelief. Words came out of his mouth: "I'm dreaming. I'm dreaming. This isn't real!"

"I'll bet you wouldn't even like me in my new orange bikini I just bought," Bobette sighed in a sultry voice.

Ben rubbed his eyes and said, "Try me." Evidently his mood had changed from surprise to anticipation.

Bobette picked up her bag and went into the bathroom. "Just give me a few minutes." It didn't take long at all to change into the bright-orange bikini and bra with little black fringes hanging on both. As Bobette slipped on her sexy black high heels, she was thinking, *Orange is Ben's favorite color. That's why I'm wearing this.*

Ben was sitting up in his bed. "I'm waiting."

"Here I come!" Bobette did a little dance and twirled around. "You like?"

Ben didn't answer, but his brown eyes were saying, "Yes, yes, yes!" He jumped out of bed and put his arms around her. He proceeded to undo the orange bra with the fringe and took a moment to caress her breasts; then he slowly pulled down her bottoms and carried Bobette to the bed. Not a word was said. Words were not necessary.

The lovemaking was intense. Once again, Bobette was in heaven. Afterward they just stayed in bed. Bobette hugged Ben. "I'm in heaven, and I didn't even have to die!"

"You give me too much credit."

"No, no...you are the best. Well, I've not had the experience you've had. Actually I've been quite the Puritan."

"Come here, you little Puritan. Let's see if I can turn you on again."

"I thought you didn't like me!"

"I told you a long time ago, I like you too much."

"Ben...Ben, I want to touch you like I've never wanted to touch a man."

Ben did not say a word as Bobette started demonstrating what she had just uttered. He moaned and groaned. It didn't take long at all for him to get an erection—a giant erection. Bobette couldn't believe how his huge penis fit into her vagina perfectly.

"Give it to me," she said. "Give it to me now, all of it!"

Ben was obedient; his performance was extraordinary. The two of them were exhausted and lay in each other's arms for quite a while.

It would be time to leave soon. After they tidied up and got dressed, they went into the living room and sat down in the comfortable chairs. Ben lit a cigarette. He admitted he was out of a job just then and, out of the blue, asked Bobette, "Can you support me in a way to which I'd like to become accustomed?"

"Can you support me in the way to which I am accustomed?" Bobette asked.

They both laughed at these ridiculous statements.

"Do you believe in God, Ben?" Bobette asked.

"Yes, in my own way."

"Do you believe in reincarnation?"

"Yes."

"I do too. I think I do. I've never thought about it much. Would you come to my rescue if Richard had me committed?"

"Awe, bull turkey!"

"He is always threatening me."

"Well, okay, I guess I would."

Ben and Bobette talked for some time about unimportant things. They reminisced about the many times they had spent at motels, mostly early in the morning. One time the motel had a swimming pool, and they had glorious fun in it, splashing around like kids.

The time had passed much too quickly; it was time for her to return to her family.

"Good-bye for now, Prince Charming." Bobette kissed him good-bye, forgetting that he didn't do sweet, except in bed -- with actions, not words.

"Well, you did one thing. You woke me up!" uttered Ben.

"You're terrible!" Bobette angrily replied.

Chapter 19

Time Stood Still

Several months passed by. The days were long and unfulfilling for Gloria. The hope that Ben would call faded into sheer disappointment. It was not going to happen now or ever. Life seemed to be uneventful and mundane. Gloria was partially satisfied by watching soap operas. In truth that was very depressing. She may as well have listened to Jeremy on the country-music station and called him. At least he always made her laugh. One time when they had talked, Jeremy had told Gloria he had a broken arm.

"Well, I've never had anything broken in my life except my heart," Gloria had told him.

"You got burned, didn't you?"

"And how!"

"Gloria, I keep telling you I'll make you forget about Ben."

"We'll see."

It was bowling night for Richard. Gloria accompanied him most of the time. Tonight she was not in the mood just to go and watch other people having fun.

"Richard, I'd rather attend the Astro Awareness meeting tonight at the library. It's a mind-control study and film. I really would like to see this. Would it be all right for me to go?"

"I really don't know what you see in that stuff. I guess it is okay, but be careful."

"I will. I'm always careful."

Astro Awareness meeting indeed. It was eight o'clock when Gloria arrived at the little country-music station where Jeremy was working. She parked the little sports car in the small parking area, smoothed her long blue dress, patted her hair, and got out.

Only once had Gloria been there, but she instinctively knew just where to go: in the front door and down the stairs to the broadcasting area. Was this déjà vu? There sat Jeremy at the microphone.

Gloria leaned over his desk slowly, her low-cut dress revealing a good portion of her bosom. Jeremy's eyebrows raised in surprise. He motioned for her to sit down and put his fingertips to his lips. He was signaling for her to be quiet. He was still on the air. Gloria sat down, crossed her good-looking legs, folded her hands, and began to study Jeremy.

He was tall, slim; his attire was casual. The young man began to twist in a nervous manner. Could he be intimidated? Hardly. His hair was flaming red, and so was his bushy mustache. The red hair was curly, fairly long, and exceptionally pretty.

Jeremy signed off the air for the night, wishing his listeners a very good weekend, and turned to Gloria. "Follow me. I have to do more news now." Gloria had no idea that country songs were played at night. The two of them went into a room that was outstanding in every way. Recording equipment was everywhere. The neatness was unbelievable.

Jeremy looked at Gloria. "Would you like a cup of coffee?"

Yes, please, if it isn't too much trouble."

Jeremy brought a cup of coffee. "Do you take cream and sugar?"

"No, thank you."

Jeremy switched on a recorder and began to read the news. He stood tall; his voice was splendid. There were many articles for him to read, each on a small piece of paper.

All at once it became clear to Gloria how this young communicastor could actually be in two places simultaneously. So simple. He recorded the news the night before, then it was played early the next morning while he was home in bed sleeping. Mystery solved.

Gloria remembered hearing him reading the news one morning. She had then phoned him at his home and was definitely surprised that he answered.

"Jeremy, how can you be in two places at once, the station and your home?" she had asked.

"Sweetie pie, I'm magic!"

Jeremy was so witty and clever. He made Gloria forget about her troubles. She did get the impression that he was quite intelligent. He had told her he was a Gemini. Gloria knew a lot about Geminis. There were several in her immediate family. A Gemini could be sweet one minute and sour and unpredictable the next. If Jeremy happened to be rude, which he often was, Gloria would not hesitate to scold him and tell him he needed lessons in good manners. They had had many down-to-earth conversations, some intensely intimate, always on the telephone.

Jeremy was about to conclude his recording of the news. He was a clean-cut young man and had a large ego. In one of their conversations recently, he had actually bragged about the size of his manhood. What arrogance, but he was entertaining.

The news was finished. Jeremy just stood there looking Gloria up and down. He uttered, "My God, you are really good-looking."

"Why thank you, kind sir. I forgot to tell you, I am a reincarnation of Aphrodite!"

Jeremy remembered that Gloria was a Libran. Anyone who knew the least inkling of astrology knew that a Libran was the flower child of the zodiac and good-looking, but what did Jeremy know about astrology? Nothing. His bag was communications, and he was the best next to Ben. Nobody was even half as good as Ben on the airwaves.

Jeremy did not waste a minute. He wrapped his long arms around Gloria and breathed into her ear, "Let's fuck, baby!"

He tried to kiss her; his hands were all over her perfumed body. This did not make an impression on Gloria. She literally shoved him away, growling, "Not so fast, you octopus, not in a radio station. Anyway, I haven't forgotten you've stood me up and hung the phone up on me."

"You love it and you know it, Mrs. Wet Thighs! Ha ha. That's your name because you want me, and you get wet when we talk."

"That's a slutty name, Jeremy!"

"You can be slutty just for me. As for your Ben, I told you that I will make him seem like a peanut butter sandwich after you've had filet mignon! I promise you; once you've been to my place, you'll want to return."

"Well, my young'n, when we have sex, it won't be here. I want candlelight, music, and finesse."

"Good luck, Mrs. Wet Thighs."

"You animal!"

Jeremy tried to kiss Gloria again unsuccessfully. His brown eyes sparkled with lust. He whispered in her ear, "Let's go to my place now."

Gloria had Jeremy where she wanted him. This time she was in the driver's seat. Looking directly into his eyes, she said, "Jeremy, I must get home. Besides, I forgot my diaphragm. You're just plain out of luck. Another thing: I haven't forgotten how cruel you were to stand me up. You are the only one in my life who has done that to me. Dearie, I'm callin' the shots from now on."

For once Jeremy was completely speechless. He did manage to let out a few words: "Come over. Come over soon!"

"Okay, Gemini, It'll have to be Thursday at eight o'clock a.m. Early is best for me. I can't seem to forget the distasteful way you have acted. It must stop!"

Gloria drove home quickly. When Richard got home and asked about the Astro Awareness film, she replied, "It was wonderful. I am so glad I saw it. By the way how was bowling?"

"We won."

Although Gloria had faked her nonchalance when she talked to Jeremy, in reality she counted the days until Thursday in anticipation of finally getting to know the young DJ. Jeremy was more than eager to know the real Gloria.

Richard had noticed the improvement in his wife's appearance. Her blue eyes sparkled. Her step was springier, and she made no complaints about her household duties. Richard began to show more attention and appreciation to Gloria but wondered about this sudden change. He would never know. Dr. Brahms was the only person on the earth who knew of Gloria's so-called double life. By law his lips were sealed. There was not one person for Gloria to place sincere confidence in. The thought of blackmail came to mind. No, it was best to remain quiet. Nobody would believe this saga as Gloria had always been the perfect Puritan.

What had happened to this model of pure innocence? Even Gloria could not fathom it. With Ben yes! With Jeremy it just did not make good sense. He was a narcissistic egotist from hell. What did that make her?

Chapter 20

Whipped Cream

The long-awaited Thursday finally arrived. The day began as usual for Gloria, arising at 5:00 a.m., preparing breakfast, making lunches, and getting the family off to work and school. This particular morning she had no time to have a cup or coffee or read the *Denver Post.* Instead the beauty routine took precedence, first and foremost the warm, relaxing bath, then the rest of the procedure in order to look and smell extraordinarily appealing.

Jeremy had ordered Gloria to wear a miniskirt, a blouse that opened down the front, crotchless panties, and no stockings. What nerve! Gloria had never worn a miniskirt. She did not know of anyone her age who did. She wanted to please Jeremy. Why not cater to him this once? Gloria had lost weight. The exercising and dieting had begun to pay off. Why not take advantage and show off her new figure on this important date?

Looking in her daughter's closet, she was lucky to find a miniskirt with a cute matching jacket and a low-cut blouse. Voilà—the ensemble fit perfectly. The uplifting bra she put on before the blouse did wonders. It definitely gave the illusion of her breasts being voluptuous, especially with her new love beads dangling in her cleavage.

She slipped on a pair of sexy sandals that matched the mini skirt and jacket perfectly. She had hidden her crotchless panties so well that even she could not find them. Therefore she had to settle for some sexy, sheer white bikini panties. Gloria glanced at herself in the full-length mirror. The image was unbelievable. It did not look like her at all but like a young woman. Hopefully Jeremy would be quite pleased.

Gloria ran to her car and scooted in quickly. She was hoping none of the neighbors saw her. It would take a while to get to Jeremy's apartment. As she drove she recollected some of their phone conversations. Jeremy delighted in obscene calls. At first they were not appreciated and too shocking. It was hard to believe that Gloria was so unsophisticated and naive. As time passed his vulgarity began to seem natural and more acceptable. She had told him she had been a lady until she had started associating with the likes of him.

He had chuckled. "Bitch, bitch, bitch!"

Jeremy always said what was on his mind—always sex! He was an intellectual. Most of the time, though, he was extremely funny and made Gloria laugh. It was good to laugh and not spend so much time being sad. Once he asked Gloria outright, "What are your measurements?"

"Bust thirty-eight B, waist twenty-seven, and hips thirty-eight."

"Not bad, Mrs. Wet Thighs."

"And I don't have gray hair either, maybe one or two, and I pull them out quickly. I don't have one gray hair on my pussy."

"You probably dye it!"

It pleased Jeremy to no end when Gloria talked dirty. It turned him on. Whatever was asked of Jeremy, he had a bright answer. Gloria had asked him, "What will you do when I take my falsies off?"

Immediately he responded with, "I'll fix you….I'll take off my plastic cock."

"You really know how to hurt an old lady, don't you?" She had reminded him that she had been engaging in sexual intercourse for more years than he had been living.

Laughing wickedly, he replied, "The older the violin, the sweeter the music."

Gloria could stop reminiscing now about Jeremy's quick wit. She was behind the apartment house. It didn't take long to get up the long flight of stairs to number ten. Gloria did not knock, just walked in as she had been instructed. My God, there was Jeremy stark naked. The long love beads that hung around his neck were impressive.

Gloria smiled. "Good morning, love." She locked the door.

Jeremy walked toward her, hugged her tightly, and kissed her passionately. He smelled wonderful. As he already had said, his manhood was large, but it was hard now—pure proof of his exaggeration.

He pushed Gloria away from him. "Hey, Mrs. Wet Thighs, you look good in a miniskirt."

"Do you really mean it?"

"Of course I mean it, dummy, but let's take your clothes off. I know you'll look better without anything on!"

As Jeremy removed Gloria's jacket, his lustful eyes were practically jumping out of their sockets. He removed her blouse. Her breasts were rising and falling as she breathed heavily. Her heart pounded. In a weak voice, she said, "I'm scared, Jeremy."

"Don't be, honey, it's all right."

Jeremy went back to work undressing Gloria slowly, caressing and stroking her body. After her clothes were removed, the tension was gone. She stood on her tiptoes, put her arms around Jeremy's neck, and pressed her warm body against him. He responded eagerly. The vibrations were strong and electrifying.

Jeremy was a person who bluntly said what was on his mind, no beating around the bush. The ambiance had disappeared. In an ugly voice, right out of Jeremy's mouth, came the unmistakable words, "Suck my cock!"

"Let's get in the mood first, please," said Gloria.

"No, suck it!" It was a demand—more like a threat.

"Right here in your living room, not your bedroom?"

"Here, *right now.*" Jeremy was impatient. He stood tall. Anticipation was overcoming him; his manhood was gigantic. "Suck it, babe. Suck it now....For Christ's sake, suck it!"

Gloria began by kissing his slim, good-looking legs, working slowly up to his thighs, and then fondled his testicles. Finally her small and delicate mouth was tasting his huge, throbbing penis, sucking gently. Jeremy groaned with pleasure as he pushed more of his pulsating penis into Gloria's mouth.

"Open your mouth more, and don't bite me. If you do, I won't fuck you." Jeremy was twisting and turning in rhythmic movements that were getting stronger and violent.

"Ah...ahh...it feels so good...ah...ahh...ooh, it feels so g-good! G-o-o-o-o-d!"

Gloria did not know how to perform fellatio, but Jeremy was completely unaware of the fact. In reality Gloria had always been passive. The concept today was that women enjoyed sex as much as men.

Jeremy was beyond excitement. Breathing hard he ordered, "Put it all in your mouth—all of it!"

Gloria honestly tried. It was just too big. She gagged and was on the verge of just plain throwing up. Jeremy had calmed down by that time and showed a bit of concern. He took Gloria's tearful and scared face in his hands. "Well, Mrs. Wet Thighs, you don't give a blow job worth a damn."

Jeremy wiped away her tears, telling her he would be only too glad to give her lessons in the future.

Gloria frowned. "I didn't know there was such an art to it. I really didn't. I am so sorry that I failed so miserably."

Jeremy simply laughed, then the two of them laughed together. Gloria took his hands in hers, leading him to the bedroom. It was very neat and tidy, which gave Gloria a good feeling.

"Maybe I can do better in the bedroom," she said.

Jeremy liked the sound of her sultry voice and pulled her down on his bed. "Do you want me to fuck you with a banana?"

"No, Mr. Filthy McNasty, the conventional method will be just fine."

"As long as you call me Mr. Filthy McNasty, I am going to fuck your ass, honey!"

"Jeremy, I'm not that sophisticated yet, you pervert."

Gloria bit him easily on the ear, pulling him on top of her. She ran her long fingers through his red mustache.

"Do you know what they say about a man with a mustache, Jeremy darling?"

Jeremy raised one eyebrow, breathing into Gloria's ear. "What do they say about a man who sports a cookie duster?"

Laughing all the time, Gloria told him, "They say he loves to eat pussy!" She ran her fingers through his thick red hair.

Jeremy said, "I have one more question for you. What do they say about a man who has a clear complexion?"

This was interesting. "What, my love, what?"

"They say he is getting plenty!"

Gloria giggled and wiggled closer to Jeremy and squeezed him. Impulsively, and feeling quite wicked now, she whispered in his ear, "I think I'm going to bite your big dick!"

This kind of talk was music to Jeremy's ears. He warned her, "You'd better not, or I won't fuck you!" He got up and left the room.

As Gloria lay there, she wished she hadn't failed so miserably at the fellatio. It occurred to her why men hired prostitutes.

Jeremy pranced back in the room with a wild gleam in his sexy brown eyes. He held up his hand and showed it to Gloria. "My dear Mrs. Wet Thighs, get ready to be sprayed with whipped cream because I am going to eat you up."

Gloria stretched out full length and saucily purred, "Spray me, Mr. Filthy McNasty, sex fiend."

Jeremy pushed the whipped cream canister's button; out squirted the whipped cream. It was so cold. "Want some on your titties?"

"Uh-huh."

Her nipples were well covered.

"Do you want some on your cunt?"

"Yes, yes, Jeremy." The cold whipped cream made contact. Gloria hugged him. "Jeremy, I lust you."

"No, darling, you lust *for* me."

"Wrong. I lust you."

By that time the two of them were covered with the whipped cream. Jeremy gave Gloria a fantastic massage all over her body, not forgetting to check to see if the diaphragm had been inserted. He thought of everything. He took a dollop of the whipped cream on his finger and slowly put it in her mouth and then in her ears. His mouth found her breast.

"Do you want me to suck your tits?" This nasty conversation was a turn-on for Jeremy.

"Oh yes, yes. Suck them. Suck them hard. It will turn me on."

First Jeremy licked the whipped cream off Gloria's little pink nipples. His face was covered.

Gloria giggled. "Hello, Santa Claus."

He sucked each breast alternately and hard while he tenderly massaged them. Gloria twisted and turned, groaning as she never had before. She took a firm hold of his hard penis and held on tightly. It did feel good. Not to be outdone, Jeremy's long fingers were digging into her vagina, tickling her, while his huge penis was still being held and massaged.

Jeremy was enjoying things. He put his tongue inside Gloria's ear, then asked, "Can I put my finger in your ass?"

"Whatever pleases you; I'm yours."

It pleased him. He did as he had requested. Actually the sensation was not unpleasant for Gloria. Jeremy looked at his willing partner lustfully, put his mouth on her breast, and sucked unmercifully hard.

Gloria put her hands on his face. "Honey, stop. You are going to suck my little titty right off my chest."

Reluctantly Jeremy stopped and looked into her beautiful blue eyes, hugged her, and whispered into her ear, "Mrs. Wet Thighs, I'm ready to eat your pussy. I hope your thighs are wet."

"Yes, they are. When I think of you, they get juicy."

Jeremy's hot fingers found the inside of Gloria's vagina and began to play. Then, in a few moments, he put some whipped cream from his hot fingers into her mouth.

"Now…now I'm going to eat your pussy."

At first things were gentle while Jeremy licked the whipped cream from her body, kissing her naval and belly. He finally kissed her where he had promised. He went wild by sucking, nipping, licking, and kissing. Gloria couldn't help but enjoy this experience. It was sexy, dirty, and downright thrilling. She groaned in delightful pleasure. When Jeremy was finished, he kissed her on the mouth. His face was white and sticky. He gave big, juicy French kisses to his willing partner.

In a sultry voice, he whispered into Gloria's ear, "Spread your legs all the way. You're getting all nine inches of my crown jewels. Are you ready, Mrs. Wet Thighs? You're going to get the fuck of your life!"

"Oh, Mr. Filthy McNasty, fuck me. Fuck me. Fuck me before I die!"

Jeremy mounted Gloria. His oversize penis slid into her vagina like a dream come true. He was having the time of his life thrusting in and out, pumping vigorously. Teasingly he would stop; then Gloria would contract her pelvic muscles while kissing and caressing this wild man.

"You little fox. I'm about ready to come," he said.

Jeremy continued for a few more moments, pumping, thrusting, and cooing nasty words to Gloria. His second wind was coming; the thrusting and pumping grew more vigorous than before. Gloria was in heaven and thought she must have been dreaming.

Gasping and shaking, Jeremy shouted, "I'm coming. I'm coming, you little fox!"

The semen gushed out, inside of Gloria and everywhere about. Jeremy shook with pleasure and pure exhaustion. He was still for a while and closed his eyes. He felt his brow being kissed.

"Jeremy, do you know you have just used up more energy to fuck me than if you'd played eighteen holes of golf?" Gloria asked.

Grinning, Jeremy responded, "Let's play some more golf."

He actually meant what he said. His erection was beginning to show. He took Gloria in his arms. "One more fuck before you have to leave."

"Are you sure? I wouldn't want to die."

"Oh, but what a way to go!"

Jeremy performed expertly again. It was amazing and unbelievable. This time really did exhaust him. The two of them lay in each other's arms for some time. Sleep was about to overcome this young stallion.

He rubbed his eyes and looked into Gloria's big blue eyes. "I think you should go now."

"It's neat, Jeremy."

"What's neat?"

"You and me, that's what. Why, I'm old enough to be your mother."

"You talk too much. Get up."

Ignoring him, she went on, "Jeremy, we didn't have candlelight and music."

"Not in the daytime, babe. Next time."

Gloria pouted a bit but got up and washed and dressed while Jeremy made a pot of coffee. He brought her a cup of it before her departure.

"Do you like me, Gemini?" Gloria asked.

"You're good-looking."

"Well, what do you think of me?"

"You're a good fuck, and I want to see you tomorrow."

"I want to, Mr. Filthy McNasty, but it's impossible to get away two days in a row. I'll take a rain check, though."

Gloria kissed her young lover good-bye. Driving home she felt the day had been pure magic, though not really at first. There was so much to learn. Jeremy had said he would be very happy to teach her. He said he would unfrustrate her. Jeremy had kept the promise this very day, although he did mention that *unfrustrate* was definitely not a word.

All the way home, Gloria thought how bad she had been today, but don't you have to be bad to be good?

Chapter 21

Reflections of Days Passed

Gloria's fun ended. The exciting days were a thing of the past. Jeremy had silently and secretly disappeared, no explanation or correspondence. It was a mystery that was never solved. Maybe he married his girlfriend, Jordan.

Jeremy's endless obscene phone calls were not missed. In all the dates, the whipped-cream episode was the most enjoyable and the nastiest. The two of them had carried on for over a year, once or twice a week. It did seem that Jeremy had thought Gloria a fun playmate and different in many ways from his young female acquaintances. Although he was entertaining, at times he could be extremely rude. Jeremy seemed to delight in Gloria's naïveté.

Often, when Gloria was relaxing, drinking a cup of coffee, she would reminisce about her experiences with the man who was twenty-two years younger than she and wondered if she were ever in Jeremy's thoughts.

On one date, at Jeremy's request, Gloria had put on a stylish trench coat without a stitch of clothing underneath, buttoned it up all the way, and donned a pair of black high heels. The weather was sunshiny and definitely favorable. When Gloria arrived Jeremy took one look and quickly unbuttoned the trench coat and pulled it open. His brown eyes sparkled with anticipation and lust.

"Come here, you little sexpot! I can't believe you actually came here like that."

It only took a few seconds for Jeremy to rip off his T-shirt, shorts, underpants and sandals. It was not a wham, bam, thank you ma'am. Jeremy was quite delighted and forgot to be rude or insulting. Coffee even was offered to Gloria before it was time to depart.

This had been a very good date. Gloria had had the foresight to bring extra clothes and shoes to wear on the way home.

No one but no one would have believed these actions of this middle-aged housewife who was just plain bored with her mundane everyday life. Gloria could not believe it herself. She thought surely she was dreaming.

Some dates had been good; others could have been called wasted time. One time Gloria had visited Jeremy without an invitation. Her surprise visit had turned out to be thoroughly wild and enjoyable.

Another date had begun well. The sun was shining; the birds were singing; all seemed well with the pleasures of extracurricular activities. Gloria and Jeremy met at a motel that was not close to either of their homes. Greetings and pleasantries were exchanged, and they had their magnificent sex orgy. Then a strange thing happened. Jeremy literally pushed Gloria out the door. It was more than rude; it was unforgiveable.

Being no dummy, Gloria put two and two together. She screamed at Jeremy, "You little bastard! You've got someone else coming here."

Jeremy had a wicked smirk on his face.

With hurt feelings and dismay, Gloria drove away. Later she thought she should have stayed right there in the parking lot to see who had entered Jeremy's harem.

There was one date where Jeremy had paid Gloria for sex. That was a twist of reality—not the ordinary. On another date the two of them had a slight disagreement over something trivial. Jeremy had the gall to say, "Well, at least I'm not charging you!" Did he think he was God's gift to women? Oh…ew! And he called his privates his "crown jewels."

Jeremy always had a big boil on his back. That was worrisome. Boils are caused by staph infections, a pus-filled inflammation under the skin. Otherwise he was perfectly clean and groomed to perfection. But that boil was so ugly, it was scary!

Life was different now and getting back to normal. It was not full of wonder and excitement, and no secret meetings. Gloria's thrills would have to be in her dreams. Perhaps, as had been suggested a few times, she should improve her marriage.

The talk shows and country-music station were a thing of the past. Contemporary music or big-band was tuned in on the radio now. One station gave prizes in contests now and then. That seemed to be Gloria's forte for the time being. Now and then she was lucky enough to win a prize. One was two tickets to watch the Globetrotters—front-row seats too! She really enjoyed that basketball game. Another prize was dinner at Chubby's Restaurant, where the Italian food was remarkable.

Life had to get back to normal. There had to be a way, but what was it? It would not be easy. The old saying "variety is the spice of life" did not seem to make an impression anymore. Gloria wondered if her secret affairs had made her any less of a respectable person or wiser in the ways of life. What would God think? A punishment would surely be awaiting her. This occupied her mind frequently.

As time passed, Gloria's indiscretions seemed to have faded away. She began working a part-time job at a candy store to fill the void. Many of the customers preferred Gloria to wait on them. One of the gentlemen customers said she was like a breath of fresh air. A very old gentlemen said this to her every time she waited on him: "My, but you have a mighty fine head of hair!" He admired Gloria's thick, long, curly brown hair. His admiration gave a glow to Gloria's self-esteem. Another old customer loved to tease Gloria. He always said to her, "Here comes trouble!"

A lady customer once said, "You look just like my friend in California—exactly like her."

Gloria smiled. "Well, they say we all have a twin somewhere. Maybe it's true."

Richard used to love Gloria's hair. He would run a hairbrush through her long, thick hair. Those were the good old days. Ben or Jeremy never would have thought to do that. If the pros and cons were measured, Richard would be ahead of them both in most things. It was time for Gloria to count her blessings, to forget about the past, and to hope that God would forgive her.

It would have been helpful if Gloria's brain would stop thinking about the past; maybe then she would have been able to get a full and restful night's sleep. As a teenager sleep had been one of her great priorities. It had been written that sleep was the key to the fountain of youth. Gloria had good genes from both her parents. They always looked much younger than they were. Luck was on Gloria's side. Her looks were deceiving. She looked fairly young.

Gloria reflected on her childhood, which had been average; although she was an only child. That had not been to her liking; she had always felt cheated. A brother or sister would have been nice. Gloria had had one very close girlfriend. The two had been like sisters. They had met when they were only twelve years old. They had lived in the same neighborhood and became friends instantly. Gloria was one year older than Margie Mae, who had had the luxury of attending a Catholic school, and she had always been ahead in her studies even though she had been a whole grade behind Gloria.

In the summer they had gone swimming every day at Washington Park. All the neighborhood kids went. Such good times they'd had. In the winter Margie Mae and Gloria had gone ice skating every night at Washington Park. It was unbelievable that this had all been free. There had been a concession stand where one could buy snacks. Washington Park had not been too far away from their homes. Most of the time the kids had walked there.

Margie Mae's parents, Mr. and Mrs. Harris, had treated Gloria like one of their own and called her their "other daughter." Mr. Harris had always said this to Gloria: "Where have you been all my life?"

Gloria had always replied, "I haven't!" This was kind of a joke between them.

Mr. and Mrs. Harris had always invited Gloria to go with them to visit their cabin in the mountains. It was not a grand cabin, but it was warm and comfortable. Gloria loved to watch Mrs. Harris make a fire in the old coal stove. There was an old man, their uncle, who was there often. When asked how he was, he always replied, "I'm sick a bed two chairs."

Gloria had so many loving memories of Margie Mae and her dear family. One bit of knowledge was not so loving. In fact it just blew Gloria's mind. Margie Mae had told her that her dad, Mr. Harris, had a girlfriend. Oh no! How could this have been true? Margie Mae's parents' marriage had been made in heaven.

When the two friends both had gotten married, they hadn't spent much time together but had kept in touch and wrote letters. When they were kids, they had dressed alike. They had made identical torso skirts. It had been quite the fashion then. Gloria had envied Margie Mae's good shape, and Margie Mae had envied Gloria's good looks. They had often joked about it. Mrs. Harris had always said, "Beauty is as beauty does."

The Harris family had been quite religious. Gloria had gone to the Catholic Church with them every Sunday. The church had been so beautiful, it took her breath away. Becoming a Catholic had been Gloria's ambition, but her father had warned her, "Not over my dead body." That was that!

In later years Gloria's father had remarried, much to her dismay. His bride was a Catholic. He had turned to that religion and begged Gloria to do the same.

"Definitely not!" Her answer had been emphatic. One might say it was pure sour grapes.

The years flew by, and one day Gloria received the bad news that Margie Mae had passed away unexpectedly. It was unbelievable. She wasn't that old. Cancer had overtaken her. *My God*, Gloria thought, *why hadn't Margie Mae let her best friend know she was sick?* Gloria could not understand.

Things were never the same after that. Hopefully the two friends would meet in heaven on a glorious day. Undoubtedly Margie Mae would be there, and Gloria hoped and prayed she would be…but…would she?

Chapter 22

A Strange Use for a Giant Gong

Dinner was over. Each member of the family was busy with his or her own interests. Gloria had just finished the kitchen duties. Life was halfway pleasant. Although it was the first of October, the weather was still summery and beautiful.

The phone rang, disturbing the peaceful atmosphere. It was a long distance call for Richard. He was in the garage working on his car as usual. Reluctantly he sauntered into the house to answer the phone. It was his niece from Nebraska. Gloria was not interested in their conversation. She knew it meant company was coming and was not the least bit happy about the fact.

Richard motioned to Gloria. "Margaret wants to talk to you."

Gloria thought this was unusual and took the phone. "Hello."

"Hi, Gloria. Is it all right if I bring a friend?"

Taken aback, Gloria answered, "I really didn't know you were coming, but I guess it's okay…if she brings a sleeping bag."

"Thank you. I'll bring a sleeping bag too."

This bit of news put Gloria in a bad mood. She had just tended her baby granddaughter a week earlier for five days and nights so her daughter could go elk hunting.

Richard had gone back to the garage to work on his car. Gloria stomped out there and angrily approached him. "What's going on anyway?"

"My brother and his family are coming to visit over the three-day weekend, and Mom and Pop are coming too."

"Oh God, I've been tricked. I wasn't aware the whole tribe was coming! Why does Margaret have to bring an outsider? She knows we don't have enough room! What is the matter with her stupid parents? Seven people coming and not enough room for them…or beds…or sheets. I hate this—hate it!"

Gloria would've loved to have her mother-in-law and father-in-law visit, just the two of them, but Jake, Jessica, Jake Jr., and Margaret were definitely not to be desired. They were pains in the ass. Jake and Jessica's kids were so demanding and bratty. They both jumped when either of their kids said, "Frog." Even Richard was so relieved when it was time for all of them to leave. He and Gloria both loved Jake dearly, although he was henpecked something fierce.

Gloria stood by the kitchen sink crying softly. Richard had come back in the house with grease on his clothes. He was not like most men, who turned to jelly when their wives cried. He became angry and shouted, "You should be happy they think enough of us to come. You don't act that way when your relatives come."

"Mine only come in twos, not a whole damn army!"

The two of them shouted; their words flew at one another. The scene was becoming violent.

Richard, with a sneer on his face, shouted, "You're a mental case! You're driving me out of my mind!"

Gloria let it all out and screamed, "I'm not driving you out of your mind. It's you and your family!"

The screams penetrated the walls of the house. The neighbors could possibly hear every word. Richard must have been out of his mind because he doubled up his fist and hit her three times very, very hard. Gloria reeled and slumped down in the corner, sobbing and hating the situation with a passion.

After some time had passed, Gloria's composure returned. Richard had stormed out of the house and driven away in his treasured El Camino. It was a blessing that the kids had not been at home for the past hour.

Gloria left the house without combing her hair or putting any makeup on. She didn't know where she was going. She wanted to run away and never come back. The thought entered her mind that maybe Ben could comfort her. That was a wild thought! They hadn't seen each other in months. She had tried to contact him. He was too evasive. She had even driven by his apartment several times. She decided to try catching him at home today.

It did not take long to get there. Gloria mentally transformed into Bobette and rang the doorbell. The door opened immediately. Ben's expression turned to surprise and then anger when he saw her.

She pushed her way in.

Ben uttered, "Come in." Then he went, practically running, into the kitchen.

Hmm, maybe he's going to fix us a drink for old time's sake Bobette thought. *Maybe he's going to be nice for a change.*

All of a sudden, a loud, thundering, booming, and clanging noise penetrated the entire apartment building. What was it? Ben had just struck a gigantic gong that was hanging in his kitchen. He actually pranced back to the living room where he'd left Bobette standing.

"Is that for the police?" Bobette laughed haughtily. Ben had warned her that he would call the police if she came to see him.

"No," Ben replied with an air of arrogance. He was quite pleased with himself. The television was blasting away, and he asked Bobette to sit down. "This program is almost over."

She sat down on the couch and was happy to be beside Ben even if he wasn't the Prince Charming she knew he could be. Ben was entirely engrossed in the TV.

Suddenly the door opened; there was no knock. In walked a huge hulk of an Amazon woman! She was fat and sloppy with stringy hair and had on glasses—definitely a first-class slob! Who in the world could she have been?

Bobette could not believe what she saw. What had happened to Ben's taste? Was this ugly pig living with him? Bobette wanted to run away. She was completely crushed. How could he....How could he? All he had to do was crook his little finger and Bobette would kiss his feet! The fact that she was married and had five children didn't enter her head.

She yelled at Ben, "You're afraid of me!" She yelled again, only louder, "*You are afraid of me!*"

Ignoring Bobette's outburst, Ben offered, "This is Harriet. Her parents are living with me."

Bobette was simply speechless, which was most unusual because as a rule she was never at a loss for words. She couldn't believe the apartment. She could see the kitchen from the living room. It was cluttered with dirty dishes and very untidy—not like Ben at all.

Big, fat Harriet waddled to the kitchen and made some drinks. She offered one to Bobette.

"No thanks," Bobette said. "I would like a cup of coffee. Do you have any?"

"I'll see if there's any left from breakfast." Harriet waddled to the kitchen again and replied, "Nope, there's not."

Ben was busy, still engrossed in the television program, ignoring both Bobette and Harriet.

The TV program finally ended, and then a phone rang. What a colossal liar Ben was. He had told Bobette that he didn't have a phone. This call was from an old friend who kept Ben on the phone for thirty-five minutes. Ben was everybody's psychiatrist and had a reputation for giving his many friends advice. The sad thing was he couldn't handle his own problems and emotions. He wouldn't even be platonic friends with Bobette. "You have to be cruel to be kind," he had told her a long time ago. They had never really talked about problems. They were too busy making love, and time was all too short.

Ben talked on and on with his friend, being so sympathetic. Harriet reached over to the couch where Ben was now sprawled and reached deep into his shirt pocket very possessively. She pulled out a book of matches and lit her cigarette. Bobette could see "Virgo" in large print on the matches.

"Are you a Virgo?" Bobette asked.

"No, I am a true Scorpio. All the Scorpio things fit me to a tee!" Harriet kept on talking. "I cook dinner one night and do the dishes, and Ben does it the next night."

Bobette was more than nauseated by Harriet's bragging but was so jealous of her. *Why am I jealous of her?* she thought. *My God…look at her fat fingers with all the gaudy rings, and her fingernails are the dirtiest. Ugh, disgusting. Positively unsanitary!*

Bobette finally realized what the gong was all about. It was to signal Harriet to come running to save Ben! Was Harriet living with him? Bobette's thoughts were getting muddled. Was the gong Dr. Brahms' idea?

Perhaps Ben was reading Bobette's mind. "No, she doesn't live with me," he said. Bobette had not asked that question, but her eyes betrayed her. It was good that Ben did not know the rest of her thoughts; he may have ordered her to leave his apartment at once.

How could Ben have stooped so low? Bobette could not believe that Harriet was a true Scorpio, the sexiest of the zodiac. There must have been negative factors in her horoscope that contradicted her Scorpio sun. She sure didn't look like a sexual come-on. "Yuck" was the adjective that came to Bobette's mind. Harriet looked as if she needed a good bath.

The conversation was not stimulating. Bobette's mind was confused. What was Harriet to Ben?

Ben took Bobette's purse from her gently. "May I?"

"It's okay. What are you looking for, a gun? Or a harem outfit? Maybe my toothbrush?"

Ben and Harriet laughed heartily.

Tears were streaming down Bobette's face. "I'm having a houseful of unwanted company in three days. I'm so upset."

Harriet puffed away on a cigarette, and her rolls of fat were bulging through her white T-shirt, which fit her like a tight glove. She smirked as words rolled out of her mouth: "Ben and I have helped each other many times."

Why in the world didn't Bobette ask, "Just how have you helped each other?"

Harriet went on and on. "When I get enough of Ben, I tell him to leave me alone."

"How can you say that? I think he's wonderful!" said Bobette.

"Easy."

Words flew, and things were getting nasty. The more Harriet spoke, the more Bobette disliked her—not dislike but pure hate.

Ben interrupted them and looked directly at Bobette. "I'm not going to break up a marriage. I'm not!"

"Ben, you can't break up something that's been dead for years. I hate him. I hate him. Have you ever lived with someone you hated?"

Harriet spoke. "Ben, I'll leave if you want me to."

"No, I want you to stay. We're friends. It's all right."

Bobette yelled at Harriet, "Why don't you go? I came to talk to Ben, and if you had an ounce of decency, you'd leave! Don't you know it's very embarrassing to me for you to be here? I want to talk to Ben alone!"

Ben insisted that Harriet stay. Was he that afraid of Bobette? Was that good or bad?

Bobette was sobbing uncontrollably and reached for a soiled Kleenex lying on the table.

Ben looked at her. "Don't use that! I used that to clean my guppies."

"You don't have any guppies."

Ben took Bobette's arm and pulled her up from the couch. "Bobette, it's late. You'd better go home and start getting ready for your company."

She jerked away from him. "Did you think I was going to stay until then? That's three days away." The thought had occurred to her to ask if she could stay for a few days, but she did not know about Harriet and her parents' situation with Ben. At that point she did not care if her marriage broke up. Her mind was not working clearly. If Harriet lived downstairs, and her parents lived upstairs with Ben, it just didn't make sense.

Ben was trying to show the door to Bobette, and Harriet had to say, "Bobette, I wanted to meet you, but I can't say I am happy to have met you."

"Why did you want to meet me? Why? So you could see what kind of a freak I am to throw myself at Ben?"

"I wanted to meet you because Ben has told me about you."

Bobette was not impressed and responded, "Well, I'm not happy to meet you either. Ben has not told me about you, and…and…you should have had the decency to leave!"

Ben was really frightened by that time and did not want the two to get into a physical confrontation. He turned to Bobette. "You should go see Dr. Brahms."

"Oh Ben, that shrink does me more harm than good! Do you know what he told me?"

"What?"

"He told me you were living with someone and had two girls on the side."

Ben and Harriet roared with laughter.

"Yes, and he told me that the reason you went to bed with me was because of my vocabulary….My vocabulary!"

Ben and Harriet couldn't stop laughing, but Bobette was still crying. "Harriet, I am sorry. I hope we meet again under different circumstances." Ben and Harriet accepted her apology. Bobette looked into Ben's eyes. "Well, Ben, the least you can do is walk me to my car."

"Okay. Let me get my shoes on first."

Ben and Bobette walked slowly down the apartment stairs and out to the street where the car was parked.

Ben quietly said, "It's late."

Bobette threw her arms around him. He was so devastatingly handsome. The hair on his chest protruded through his unbuttoned shirt. The moon shone brightly—it was a gorgeous night. "Ben, if you don't want to break up my marriage, why can't we just play around? We've not been caught yet."

"No" was Ben's emphatic reply. His arms hung limply at his sides. He just wanted her to leave.

"Won't you kiss me good-bye? Ben, Ben, you're the best thing that has ever happened to me. You really are." Tears were streaming down her face. She was embarrassed by her violent show of emotion. "You are the best thing that's ever happened to me!"

Ben quietly answered, "Thank you, thank you."

Bobette laid her head against his shoulder. "Ben, time is so short. I love…I love you. You've got ice in your veins. Look at that beautiful moon. This night is made for love!"

Ben showed no emotion. He was as cold as ice. "Go…and drive carefully."

"I won't drive carefully. I won't!"

Ben helped Bobette get into her car and repeated, "Drive carefully."

This couldn't be real. She drove away at a moderate rate of speed. The tears were still flowing; it was a little hard to see. She had forgotten to put her glasses on. She went around the block and passed the apartment house, wanting to go in again. Her mind told her it would be futile.

Bobette, now back to Gloria, did arrive home safely. The family was not up; everyone was in bed asleep, and that was pure luck—no explanations to make. Coffee would be good to soothe her jangled nerves. The coffeepot was able to make just one cup. Gloria's astrology magazine was on the table.

"Hmmmmmm, I wonder what it says for Libra." She opened to the page for Libra, the scales. It read:

> This month begins on a tense note as the full moon generates some sort of a showdown between you and someone close to you. Avoid becoming too emotional about it all. The full moon tells you to take it easy; don't be prodded into doing or

saying something you will regret. Valued relations could be a
little strained.

Gloria had mistakenly thought the full moon would've been to her advantage. She finally managed to go to sleep, but her ears kept ringing with Ben's words: "Drive carefully!"

Chapter 23

Unexpected Phone Call

Life was going well lately—surprisingly better than ever. Gloria was doing what her husband expected of her. The children were growing up and doing well in school. Only two of them were still at home. Clarissa had received an "excellent achievement" award, which was an incentive for her younger brother. Gloria had always been a room mother for her youngest child. She did not delegate duties to the other mothers in the class as she would rather do them herself. That way she knew the job(s) would get done well. For special occasions Gloria baked cupcakes or cookies. So many of the room mothers didn't bake and would simply buy cupcakes or cookies from the grocery store. Gloria loved to surprise the class with her special home-made treats. This was a job that was a pleasure. The teachers appreciated her efforts.

David's class went on field trips now and then. Gloria, being an overly protective mother, insisted on going with them. At first the teacher disapproved royally of Gloria's presence but found out that she was more of a help than a hindrance. Gloria was always invited after that first field trip. Persistence had paid off.

Life was getting back to normal. A few years had magically gone by. Gloria was behaving herself.

One day she had been out doing some errands and going to the grocery store. Groceries seemed to have higher prices each day. There were not a lot of things to bring in. As she was unloading the groceries, she noticed a note by the telephone. Evidently one of the kids had written it.

"Who called?" Gloria yelled at Clarissa.

"Don't know, Mom. It was some man. He wanted you to call him."

"I don't have time now to call anybody now. It's probably just a salesman."

Gloria put the few groceries away. It wasn't time to start preparing dinner. David and Clarissa were involved in a TV show. The children had done their homework—mother's orders.

Maybe I'll make that call. Can't imagine who would call me. Gloria dialed very slowly. The phone rang several times. She was impatient.

Finally, a deep voice answered, "Hello."

Gloria thought she would surely faint, barely getting the words out. "Not Ben!"

"Yes."

"Are you trying to trick me? You are tricking me! What do you want?"

"I just want to talk to you."

"I don't believe you. I just don't believe you. Why are you calling me? What's the catch?"

"No catch, Bobette. I have really missed you and want to see you."

"Bobette died a long time ago, you know that."

"Perhaps I can make her come back to life."

"So you can make me die again?"

After a little more conversation, plans were made to meet at Civic Center Library in the children's section on the following Friday. This was Wednesday.

Gloria's thoughts were overwhelming. *Why in the world should she waste her time on Ben? Why didn't she hang up on him and tell him to get lost?* Her life was back on an even kilter.

Friday arrived. Gloria/Bobette was still hesitant about going to the library. This meeting did not have the excitement or expectation of other times. The weather was sunshiny and pleasant. The drive was short as the library was close to Gloria's home. There were not many cars in the parking lot—a plus. One of Gloria's neighbors could've been there. She got out of the car, locked it, looked around, and then slowly walked into the library and found the children's section. Thank goodness the children were all at school. There was only one soul sitting there at a table reading a book.

Bobette pulled out a chair and sat down beside Ben. "Hello, stranger," she barely whispered.

"Hello yourself," Ben replied in his low, sexy voice. "Let's get out of here, okay?

"Where?"

"I have a motel room rented."

The two of them sauntered out to the parking lot.

Ben said, "Follow me. It's fairly close, and we can park out back."

They got into their own cars and drove slowly, and Bobette wondered why in God's name she was doing this. Was the devil making her do it?

It didn't take long to get to the motel—Shady Comfort. The parking lot was quite secluded with large, leafy maple trees surrounding it and the building. Ben took Bobette's hand, leading her to room number six—that definitely had to be a good omen. Feelings swept over her. Ben unlocked the door, still holding her hand, they entered the room and he quickly locked the door. The blinds were already pulled down, making it somewhat dark. No words were spoken. Ben unbuttoned Bobette's sheer blouse. His eyes lit up.

'No bra?"

"No bra…just for your pleasure."

"I love your breasts. May I touch them?"

"Go ahead. You know how that turns me on."

Ben massaged her breasts so tenderly and kissed them, then he led Bobette to the bed. He undressed her, full of anticipation, and ripped off his clothing

"Lie down, Bobette. Let me taste your beautiful breasts." Ben did taste them one after another and began sucking them vigorously.

"Oh, ooh, Ben, you know I love it. You know how to turn me on!"

"They are so sensual."

Bobette was trembling with excitement while Ben fondled her clitoris. He was a real gentleman; he would never say "tits" or "pussy." He had informed Bobette, during one of their informal little talks, that he was born under the sign Clitoris.

All the time Ben was giving Bobette such pleasure, she had a firm hold on his solid erection, his amazing manhood. Ben was smiling as Bobette squeezed his penis and went up and down, fondling him, even gently squeezing his scrotum. Heavens, his balls were huge. What a man!

Bobette, flat on her back now, spread her legs wide open. "Do you want me, my Prince Charming?"

"Yes, my little vixen, my little she-devil, I want you. It's been too long since we've made love."

Ben crawled on top of his willing partner and, slowly teasing her, went in and out of her pulsating vagina. Bobette put her hands on his head and pulled him down, kissing him softly. Suddenly Ben's tongue was in her mouth. Without hesitation she began to French kiss him. It was exhilarating. Her passion excited Ben to no end. He took Bobette to heavenly heights. He loved her response. All this time he was giving thrill after thrill to her while pumping up and down vigorously.

When he climaxed, Bobette kissed him again and whispered, "Darling, I'm in heaven."

Ben was trembling. "Ah, ahhh, Bobette. I have to rest a little bit."

"Stay on top of me. Don't get off yet. You feel so good!"

Ben obeyed her wish. He was totally exhausted; he closed his eyes and went to sleep right on top of her, just like old times. Half an hour passed before he opened his eyes. He rolled over. "Time to get dressed and get back to the old grind."

The magic had vanished. It was time to return to reality. Ben looked directly into Bobette's beautiful blue eyes and said in his alluring, charismatic voice, "I'll call you."

"I won't hold my breath waiting."

Ben kissed Bobette on her cheek. They casually strolled to their cars and drove away.

There were so many questions that were unanswered. He wasn't asked how he was doing, if he was working, who he was keeping company with, and how his sex life was.

The fact that Ben and Bobette's chemistry was so electrical was terrifying. It was hot! All Ben had to do was crook his little finger, and Bobette would come running even though she had vowed to erase him from her thoughts forever. Ben was a fickle Gemini, but why in the world did he keep coming back to her? It was a mystery that could not be solved now, maybe never. Perhaps it had to be lived.

The two lovers managed to see one another once or twice a week. Bobette was under Ben's spell. He always paid for their time spent in a motel. It was sad to be there for only an hour or two when the room was paid for for a whole day and night. One time they went to the park on a lovely, sunshiny day and made love underneath a big blanket just like a couple of teenagers. It was thrilling. Bobette had never done this in her youth. She certainly forgot her age. At times Ben would go to Bobette's house when Richard was at work and the children were in school. Bobette would greet him completely naked or just in a cute little apron. This delighted Ben. Luck always seemed to be on their side. They never got caught.

One day Richard did come home when Ben was there. Bobette saw Richard's car, and then he came right inside the house.

"Oh my God, Ben. Hide. Hide in the guest closet!"

Ben scurried into the closet and pulled the clothes around him.

Richard didn't stay long. There was no reason for his coming home in the middle of the day. He found some papers he had forgotten to take to work that morning and left in a hurry. He did not even speak to Gloria.

She went directly to the closet where Ben was hiding. He was white as a ghost and said nothing but "I've got to get out of here!" He did not want a mad husband after him.

Two days passed. Ben finally called and suggested that a motel or his place would be the safest. Richard could never know about Gloria's indiscretions. What he didn't know could not hurt him.

Chapter 24

Where Did the Time Go?

Bobette and Ben had their on-again, off-again affair. It lasted only three months. Ben did his usual rejection performance. Would Bobette/Gloria ever learn? The fact was that Ben was just using her. She would feel completely destroyed and mope around for days and then come to her senses, reevaluate the positive aspects of her situation, and determine to live life respectfully and positively from that point onward. Life had already been lived to the fullest. It should have lasted for the rest of her life if only in her dreams.

Gloria's dreams were not pleasant, as in them Ben was always with another woman and escaping. The dream book she bought did not help matters either. What a terrible waste of money that was. Gloria's dreams were vexing. She would wake up each morning simply worn out. This situation had to change. Some time ago, before their last breakup, Gloria had talked to Ben. He had informed her that he and his companion were living together and that it would probably be a permanent arrangement.

Gloria had asked him, "And...how is your sex life with her?"

"Mild. Just mild."

Gloria was very sure this new arrangement would not last even though his woman was well to do and had a very nice condominium.

Many years had passed. Gloria, by that time, knew that Ben was out of her life forever. She was now working full-time at the candy store. This helped considerably. The customers liked for Gloria to wait on them. She made them feel special. Her personality was like sunshine.

Richard and Gloria's children were all grown up now and had homes of their own. As a result there was more time for Richard and Gloria to pursue their hobbies or whatever interests they had. Computers seemed to be the in thing. Almost everybody owned one. Richard did not like them—said computers took away too many jobs. One day, however, he was in a very good frame of mind and surprised Gloria with a brand-new Hewlett Packard laptop. Surprises are wonderful. With the help of her kids, it didn't take her long to get the hang of it. Sometimes she would have a problem and telephone one of her children. The children were always willing to help her. Gloria had a new toy. It did occupy her time. In fact Richard wondered why he had ever bought it and said it was *too addicting*.

Learning the computer was not an easy task, especially for an older person. Gloria did have many problems learning how to use the computer. When things didn't go just right, Richard would say, "What have you done to it now?" Although he had no interest in the computer, he had hooked it up and got it ready to use. It was amazing how smart Richard was; he just naturally knew how something should work. The instruction booklet was of some help to him, but he was naturally gifted in so many fields—electronics, plumbing, mechanics. He could fix anything at home. He was a true handyman.

Many times Richard would assemble things from kits. One time he put a pinball machine together. It turned out perfectly. The entire family loved it. Richard could listen to a car motor and say what was wrong with it. The family and neighbors always asked for his advice, even about their lawnmowers. A close neighbor would bring his lawnmower over and say, "Listen to this, Richard, and tell me what's wrong with it."

When there were problems, Gloria could rely on one of her kids to come to her aid. She would tell them her computer had a mind of its own. "If I breathe too hard, it deletes my work." She was told not to drag her fingers. That was a definite help. There were so many things to know and learn. Having a brand-new computer was thrilling. Her kids were her teachers, so she did not have to go to school to learn the basics. When Gloria was baffled by a question, she found the answer on her new toy. Even Richard seemed to appreciate it when Gloria found out something he wanted to know.

David was the only one of Gloria's children who didn't own a computer. He was familiar with them, though, and visited his parents often. He was welcome to use the computer. He was a whiz on it and always looked up prices of car parts or tools. Richard still moaned that computers put too many people out of work. He was right. His sister refused to learn how to use the computer at her job as a bookkeeper. Many people felt that computers were not there to stay. Little did they know!

The candy store where Gloria worked had cut the hours of its employees but expected the same amount of work from them as before. That did not make sense to the employees. It did to the boss.

On one ordinary day, Gloria was waiting on customers at the candy store. There was a man waiting to be helped. His cap covered his gray hair. He had a gray beard with a little black running through it.

"May I help you, sir?" Gloria asked.

"You certainly may, Bobette!"

Gloria/Bobette couldn't believe her ears and almost fainted. She looked directly at the customer. "Ben, Ben....Tell me you aren't Ben!"

"In the flesh."

"How did you know I work here?"

"I have my ways."

"Since you're a prospective customer, I suggest you buy some candy so we won't attract undue attention. What would you like?"

"You pick it out for me. I'll trust your judgment."

Bobette picked out some dark chocolate and some light chocolate and rang it up on the cash register. As she handed Ben the little white sack, he took hold of her hands and squeezed them very tightly. Looking into her eyes, he asked, "Do you have a computer?"

"Why yes, yes I do. Haven't had it very long. Would you like my e-mail address?"

Ben let go of Bobette's hands when the other clerk came out to check if there were any more customers. In a very low voice, Ben answered, "I would love it."

Bobette tore off a piece of paper from a little pad sitting on the counter, wrote down the information, and handed it to Ben. As he was leaving, she said, "Have a nice day."

Bobette was dumbfounded and assumed her mind was playing tricks on her. Had she really seen Ben? It must have been wishful imagination. That must have been it.

The other clerk, Nadia, asked, "Who was that man?"

"Oh, just my neighbor. He just found out I work here. Probably thought I'd give him some free samples."

"Did you?"

"Heavens no. I don't want him to come back."

It was almost time for Gloria and Nadia to punch the time clock. The teenagers would be in to work for the next three hours. The boss favored the teenyboppers. They could get away with murder—loafing on the job, talking on their cell phones, or talking to their friends who came in the store pretending to buy something. Such was life.

Gloria looked exceptionally good in her white uniform. The dress was just a hair below her knees. Her white shoes were polished to perfection. Most of the time there was a real flower in her hair. The regular customers always complimented her and told her they liked to see her. Compliments made her feel special.

The house was quiet when Gloria arrived home. Richard was not home yet. There would be time to check her e-mail on the computer and have a cup of coffee and change clothes. Her uniform was still clean but smelled like delicious chocolate. Sometimes Gloria was able to bring home a bag of rejects—the boss demanded perfection. The marks on the chocolates had to be perfect or else they could not be sold. The rejects were called "seconds." They were just as good and tasty as the perfect ones, and they were absolutely free for the clerks.

The coffee took only five minutes to be ready. The little drip pot did a wonderful job. The computer seemed to be waiting to be turned on. It was one of the best. Gloria had a lot to learn; she had learned only the basics. She had bought a book that promised to tell a senior citizen how to do everything even if she were a complete dummy. But the book was too technical and was hard to comprehend. She returned it to the bookstore and received a full refund.

The coffee was ready. "Ah, there's something about a good cup of coffee," she said. "So relaxing." She took a few sips and turned on her computer. Yes, yes, there was something from Ben. It wasn't long, very casual and asking Gloria to e-mail him soon. She wasn't going to rush into anything too soon and scolded herself for being excited to hear from Ben. He was still with his companion and had a job. He gave no reason whatsoever as to why he had contacted her.

Gloria/Bobette and Ben e-mailed one another every single day—just small chitchat. It was inevitable that their off-again, on-again romance would be on once more.

Ben's companion did not satisfy his needs—perhaps monetarily and socially but not in the sexuality department. Truthfully the magnetic chemistry still existed between Ben and Bobette; even though they were much older by that time. Ben still held Bobette under his spell. Was it kismet?

Ben invited Bobette to his place. It really wasn't his. The condo belonged to Olivia. It was medium-size, very attractive, and in an upscale neighborhood. Huge maple trees hovered around it, and it had an enclosed backyard patio. Ben had planted many different kinds of plants. It was a beautiful sight with the multiple colors. To add to the grandeur was a large, black iron gate that led to the patio from the carport. Bobette was impressed. Ben was waiting for her at the large, iron gate, watching as she parked in the carport.

He opened the gate. "Come in."

"Is there a chance Olivia will come home from work while I'm here?"

"Not too likely. Relax."

Bobette thought Ben had a job but didn't ask him. He took her by the hand and led her through the sliding doors to the small but very neat kitchen. He locked the door and closed the drapes, then took Bobette in his arms and hugged her tightly. His hands found their way to her breasts. "I think they're bigger!"

"I've been doing bust exercises, just for you! I'm also standing up straighter. I'm so glad you noticed."

"Come on upstairs. I'll show you the bedroom."

They went up two flights of stairs. There was a king-size bed with the blankets pulled down and bright-red sheets—so eye catching. The black headboard had beautiful black-iron scrolls here and there—so artistic.

The two of them gazed into one another's eyes.

"It's been such a long time since we've seen each other, Ben."

"It's been too long, Bobette."

Gloria melted when he called her that. It seemed like old times. They wasted no time in undressing each other.

"Shall we shower first, Bobette?" Ben asked.

"We've never done that before. I'm game."

The two lovers got into the shower. Ben closed the plastic curtain that had pretty, colorful butterflies imprinted on it. He turned the water on to just the right temperature for Bobette. She preferred it a little warmer than most. Then Ben opened a bottle of lavender body wash. They enjoyed taking turns soaping each other up with lots of rubbing and body touching—oh so sexy. Ben took the handheld shower nozzle and rinsed her off very gently. He handed Bobette a large towel. They both dried themselves off quickly. Ben was such a gentlemen, always striving to please Bobette and asking, "Is this all right?"

Ben's wish was Bobette's command. Whatever he suggested, she was willing to try it. He had certainly taught her things she had not experienced before. Making love on bright-red sheets was a new experience. Ben was such an expert when it came to sex. Bobette wasn't too sure about his love. She loved him dearly and was turned on by him sexually. He had never told her that he loved her. She knew the effect she had on him was sizzling.

Today the sex was extraordinary. They made up for lost time and performed all the things Ben had taught her, naughty but nice. He gave Bobette the ultimate kiss, which was returned with enthusiasm. She squirmed and purred with his hot tongue kissing, licking, and tenderly biting her hot, undulating clitoris. Ben told Bobette she didn't have to return the favor.

Wanting to please her lover, she said, "Ben, I want to. You know I never wanted to touch a man like I want to touch you. I've told you that before!"

Ben thoroughly enjoyed having fellatio performed on him. That was something Gloria would not have thought of doing. When she was Bobette, it was a different matter. The sky was the limit. Ben did a lot of groaning and moaning with pure pleasure while Bobette stroked, kissed, and sucked his erect penis. She promised to get more efficient at it, but Ben did not complain. Bobette was in heaven when he fondled her breasts and sucked them. That was such a big thrill. At times she would be all red from his whiskers. No problem—she loved it.

It was time to stop their wonderful little orgy. They got cleaned up and dressed. Then they went out to the patio and sat in comfortable chairs, enjoying the sunlight, and visited for a short spell. Ben lit up a cigarette. He was such a health nut about his diet and ate all the right things. Didn't he know that smoking could kill a person? That subject was not mentioned. They did talk about a lot of things. The time passed all too quickly. It was time for Gloria—not Bobette now—to return to reality.

As they parted with a kiss, Ben said, "Bobette, I've had a wonderful time, but I have something to tell you next time we see one another."

Chapter 25

A Double Life

Gloria was still in suspense, wondering what Ben had to tell her. She would just have to wait. In the meantime she had something to tell him, the dream she had had last night...so surreal. Taking a chance and hoping Ben could talk without being overheard, she dialed his number.

"Hello," Ben said in his beautiful voice.

"Hello, can you talk?," Bobette whispered.

"Yes, it's all clear."

I had the best dream last night. It was your fiftieth birthday."

"That was a long time ago," Ben chuckled.

Excitedly, Bobette replied, "It was as if it had happened only yesterday.

"Okay Bobette, tell me your dream."

"I had come to your office that was in an impressive building. When I knocked on the door, you opened it and were surprised to see me. Quickly you welcomed me in, then locked the door and closed the blinds. Immediately I knelt down and pulled your pants and shorts down to your ankles. You said, "What next?" You were quite excited. I said, "Ben, I've never done this before." You said, "First time for everything." I gave you a more than satisfactory blow job. In the dream, you smiled and said, "Darling; that is the best birthday present I've ever had, and I will remember it forever. Thank you!"

Ben had listened intently to the dream and said, "I will have to have fiftieth birthdays more often!"

Since Ben and Bobette were seeing one another again, life seemed too good to be real. They were e-mailing each other every day and night. Their words were chosen very carefully and not a bit incriminating. Richard and Olivia were too busy to get on computers, so no worries in that department.

If a rendezvous were planned, on the computer Ben would type, "I need to do my shopping early, about ten in the morning." It was at Ben's place. Their shopping would last for two glorious hours. It was always an adventure to look forward to.

Gloria had often mentioned to Ben that she wanted to spend a night with him. It could have been possible but was improbable at that time.

The double life these two were leading was a miracle. Wasn't it a known fact that cheaters always got caught sooner or later? Gloria preferred a motel. That was the safest place to be and the most relaxing.

Plans were made on the computer for 9:00 a.m. one day. Getting away was easier and easier in those days. Gloria/Bobette parked in the carport.

Ben was waiting for Bobette at the beautiful, iron gate that led to the patio. "Come in, come in."

Bobette handed him a beautiful little bouquet of flowers from her very own garden. He did not thank her but took her hand as they walked into the kitchen. Ben looked around for a minute and then found a vase. He put the red roses, daisies, and miniature purple and yellow pansies in it.

"Ben, what is it you said the other day you were going to tell me?"

"Oh…that. Hm, ah. I'm not proud of it."

"What is it, sweetie?"

"Well…the reason I have to know two hours before you get here is…is that I have to take my Viagra."

"Really? I had no idea."

The two of them went upstairs to the bedroom and undressed each other, getting excited.

"Before we shower, I want you to see this." Ben handed Bobette a plastic ring and told her to slip it onto his penis. It was very tight and a little hard to get on. The plastic ring had performed its duty! Bobette uttered, "Bigger is better!"

Ben had always been well-endowed. Bobette admired him and praised him constantly. It did seem to embarrass him somewhat. They were both much older now, and age does take its toll. Bobette felt sexually reborn because Ben had introduced her to so many things. But now Ben was partial to oral sex because he felt he was not as good as he used to be. Bobette disagreed. She should have persuaded him to try a little harder.

They took their invigorating shower, rubbing together, kissing, and fondling one another. Ben's penis was outstanding and completely erect. Bobette was delighted and enamored and led him to the bed holding his wonderful manhood that never ceased to amaze her. The Viagra was working overtime. Ben tried coitus but gave up too soon. Why? Why? Why? The sheets were perfectly clean. Ben always put clean sheets on the bed for their lovemaking. He was the epitome of cleanliness, saying that cleanliness was next to godliness. Jeremy had said, "Cleanliness is next to sex!" Both her Geminis were right.

Was oral sex evil? Bobette hadn't decided. It sent her to cloud nine. Ben was delighted when Bobette returned the favor. It must have been good. Was it just plain nasty or plain thrilling? Maybe both. It led to fantastic orgasms!

Time passed all too quickly as always. Ben and Bobette had their usual chat and relaxation on the patio, talking about everything from soup to nuts. Ben smoked his usual cigarette. Bobette never chided him for smoking. It was time for her to leave.

Ben gave her a kiss on the lips. "E-mail me, okay?"

"I will tonight."

Bobette transformed back into Gloria and decided to stop at the library and get a few books on astrology so Richard wouldn't question her about the day's activities. He knew she didn't spend all day cleaning house; even though it was quite presentable.

Gloria changed clothes. She couldn't look sexy when her husband came home. He might take advantage. Dinner would be ready soon. Most of it was ready. The pork chops had been cooking in the Crock-Pot. The corn on the cob had been husked earlier and plastic wrapped and was waiting to be put in the microwave at a moment's notice. A salad and a vegetable would complete the meal. They always had milk also. Although Gloria had a sweet tooth, she had decided not to have dessert every day. Calorie watching was on her agenda besides doing some exercises.

Richard had remarked about this sudden change and asked Gloria, "Who are you trying to impress?"

"You, darling!"

Richard just snorted.

Dinner was very good. Richard had something positive to say: "I thought dinner was excellent!"

"I accept your compliment, kind sir, and I will try to make good dinners more often."

"I will probably bowl better tonight thanks to my elegant dinner."

Gloria decided her good cooking was worth the effort and planning, and it would be to her advantage to use her cooking skills again. Richard often teased her and said he had taught her everything she knew about cooking.

Gloria used to accompany Richard on bowling night. Since Ben had come into her life, she made valid excuses to stay home, claiming to be too tired or a need to study her astrology lessons. She began taking a correspondence course, which took a lot of time. Reincarnation was part of the lesson. This had never entered Gloria's mind before. The family thought she was going overboard with this concept. Maybe there was something to it. Could anyone disprove reincarnation? On the other hand, could anyone prove it? Gloria had discussed this with Ben in one of their chats. They had decided they had been lovers in a previous life.

Richard was ready to leave. "Don't you want to go?"

"No thanks. I'm rather tired."

"It isn't from cleaning house. Do you want me to give you a list?"

"Good-bye, smart-ass."

Richard smiled and picked up his bowling ball in its brand-new bag and went out the door. Gloria sat down with a hot cup of coffee, pondering. Ben was on her mind. She secretly wished they could go on a real date. In the many years, it had never happened. She had asked Ben where he might take her on a real date.

"Maybe to a ballet or a concert," He had said.

Gloria had never attended a ballet or a concert. Maybe it would be worthwhile. Basketball games were her favorite. At present she would have to be content with e-mailing Ben.

Their e-mails were just chitchat, nothing specific. That night Gloria mentioned that shopping could be on her agenda for the next day. Ben responded immediately. The "you've got mail" sounded loud and clear on Gloria's computer. The mail read, "Dear Friend, I would love to go shopping at eleven in the morning. Meet you at the usual place. We will definitely repeat our last shopping spree!"

Gloria looked forward to tomorrow but was somewhat dubious of it if Ben meant oral sex. Who was she kidding? Whatever Ben wanted he got. At least he didn't suggest whips and chains. Everything would be just plain copasetic, A-one okay. Bring it on! This double life couldn't get any better!

Chapter 26

Life Changes from the Good to the Ugly

Bobette met Ben at the agreed time and place. Unspeakable actions were performed as planned. All was going well.

"Bobette, you don't have to do this if you don't want to," he said.

"Ben...Ben, you are so good to me. I've told you before, I want to touch you like I never wanted to touch any man. The sky is the limit with you!"

Ben was absolutely touched by this confession but did not utter one word. Taking her in his arms, he kissed and hugged her with such emotion. He was trembling. "We have time now, Bobette. Shall we make love one more time?"

"Yes, yes, yes, my darling. I am willing. Take me. I am yours!"

Bobette's response made Ben smile. He led her to the bed saying, "Come to me, you little sex pervert!"

"You made me that way," Bobette informed him.

Ben was delighted by her response. Things turned hot and heavy. This meeting lasted much longer than usual. Both were in a state of euphoria. The excitement left them trembling. It was always sad when they had to part—more so for Bobette.

Ben and Bobette saw one another at least once a week for over a year. It was nice. Lady luck always seemed to be on their side, but the situation changed. Olivia became ill and was forced to quit work. This put a huge damper on the surreptitious meetings. Ben was able to stay home most of the time and care for Olivia as he wasn't working too much. The care given was conscientious, willingly, and dedicated.

Ben was not able to leave now. He had hopes that Olivia's daughter may offer to babysit now and then. In the meantime the computer was the communication between the two connivers.

Gloria hadn't heard from Ben for a few days and was getting depressed. She was delighted when she finally had a message from him. It read:

TO MY BOBETTE
A LOVE STORY

I SHALL SEEK AND FIND YOU.
I SHALL TAKE YOU TO BED AND
HAVE MY WAY WITH YOU…
I WILL MAKE YOU ACHE, SHAKE, AND
SWEAT UNTIL YOU MOAN AND GROAN.
I WILL MAKE YOU BEG FOR MERCY
AND BEG FOR ME TO STOP.
I WILL EXHAUST YOU TO THE POINT THAT YOU
WILL BE REVIVED WHEN I'M FINISHED WITH
YOU, AND YOU WILL BE WEAK FOR DAYS.

ALL MY LOVE,
THE FLU

Now, get your mind out of the gutter…and get your flu shot!

"That rascal," Gloria muttered. "It is pretty funny though."

Another message jumped up: "I remember our last shopping spree and the unspeakable actions we dared to do on that wonderful day. Hopefully we can repeat the same as soon as possible. Olivia's daughter has promised to help me now and then. I do need all the help I can get. For now we will have to be content with our memories. N'est-ce pas?

Gloria had often wondered why Ben and Olivia didn't get married. Ben never discussed his personal affairs, and Gloria never questioned him. They were always much too busy making love to have any serious conversations. When they did talk, it was idle chitchat, usually funny and so relaxing out on the patio that had so many beautiful flowers. Ben was a great gardener. In one of their talks, they decided they were soul mates. Gloria was still in la la land. It could never end. Ben rocked Gloria's world. It would be so difficult not to see him often. Patience would have to be her virtue for the time being.

Olivia had fallen and broken her hip. She would have to have a hip replacement and would be in the hospital for a week and in a wheelchair for several weeks after that. The sad situation went from bad to worse. Olivia passed away from a heart attack, unbeknownst to Gloria.

That evening at the dinner table, Richard informed Gloria that he would be going out of town, not on business but for a pleasure trip to the NASCAR races in Las Vegas. Several of the family members were also going. Richard was quite aware that Gloria would not want to go. Races were not her interest. Four days would be too much.

"Is it all right if I go, Gloria?" he asked.

"That's okay with me. You know I wouldn't enjoy all that hot sun and walking. No problem. I have more than enough to keep me busy right here at home."

Hooray, oh hooray! was the thought penetrating through Gloria's mind. *I can spend some quality time with Ben. I want to tell him right now but will have to wait and do it later when the time is right.*

A safe time arrived. Gloria turned on her computer. The message from Ben was so unexpected. It read, "Olivia has passed away due to a heart attack. I am sorry I couldn't have done a better job of caring for her….Talk to you later."

A few days passed. There was a very impressive obituary in the *Denver Post* about Olivia and her accomplishments. Gloria was surprised and tucked the obituary away. Maybe it would be all right to send Ben a bit of e-mail. It read, "Ben, I am so happy because in a few days, I will be free as a bird—free for four entire days. Can you believe it? I am sorry for the turn of events, but LIFE WILL GO ON!"

The response was immediate: "Well, I'm really busy. I have a meeting on Monday and a speaking engagement on Tuesday. Olivia's niece is coming into town, and she is going to be here for a few days."

This certainly deflated Gloria's ego; in fact it crushed it. The words from Ben were not what she had expected. Her ego had disappeared. For sure Ben had not been in love with Olivia. The computer was turned off with a thump.

Richard had told Gloria that anytime a woman threw herself at a man, he would definitely take advantage of her sexually. *So what was the matter with Ben? What kept him away from his lover?* Gloria surmised that she was his lover. On second thought, *maybe she was just his girl toy!*

Ben had told Gloria that his friends had advised him to get a life. His period of mourning was not long. He took the advice and was having the time of his life, going here and there with old friends he had neglected during the years he had been a faithful caretaker of and slave to Olivia.

Gloria felt completely forsaken. Maybe she shouldn't have been so self-centered, should have let Ben have his space. On impulse she e-mailed him. "Are you mad at me? It should be vice versa!"

They exchanged instant messages and got into a bad argument over his rejecting her. Then Gloria picked up her phone and called Ben. Words were exchanged.

"Ben, it's not like I'm moving in with you!"

Ben yelled, "Well, I never asked you to!"

Tears were streaming down Gloria's face. She slammed the phone down, almost breaking it.

Three days passed. Gloria received an e-mail from Ben:

> In some ways I seem to be going overboard trying to rebuild friendships and relationships that I necessarily neglected for so long. Please do not read any bitterness or resentment into that comment. I took care of Olivia the best I could for as long as it was necessary. I regret that I couldn't have done a better job.
>
> Now I'm rebuilding my social and professional networks. I'm also trying to deal with my self-imposed guilt and shame for not meeting my own realistic expectations.
>
> Please read no anger in this. I'm just a guy trying to do what I can in a world I never made and don't understand at all.

> Yeah, yeah I know. It's been a few days, and I've not responded to your kind thoughts. I've allowed myself to become busied with other stuff. I've been inconsiderate, and I apologize. Okay. There! End of rant!

A week or so later, Gloria found herself catering to Ben's invitation to "shop." She was excited and forgot to be mad at him.

Ben was as charming as ever and hugged Bobette—not Gloria now—so tightly when she stepped inside his door. Not a word was said. They went straight to the bedroom and took a shower together. After drying off they went to the bed with the red sheets. Ben had Bobette put the plastic ring on his penis. No mention of the sex pill was made. It did what it was intended to do. In between times Ben heated two metal balls called *executives' pacifiers*. He asked Bobette if she wanted to insert them.

"You do it for me," she replied.

Ben inserted the two very warm balls, one at a time, gently into Bobette's moist vagina. This was another completely new experience for her. She admitted that it felt very good.

Ben said, "Leave them in. They will fall out later."

Ben and Bobette got dressed and went out to have their usual chat and bask in the brilliant rays of sunshine. They talked about being older, and not as good-looking as they once had been.

Ben looked at Bobette. "It hurts, doesn't it?"

"Yes, yes, it certainly does. Ben, I have a hypothetical question for you."

"Okay, shoot."

"If I were able, would you let me move in with you?"

That certainly destroyed the pleasant atmosphere. "No, definitely not. I am not even thinking about that at this time."

Astrology specifies that Geminis shy away from emotional people. Bobette said her good-bye in tears.

Concerned, Ben said softly, "Drive carefully."

Ben always portrayed a perfect gentleman.

Chapter 27

The Last Time

The situation was getting progressively worse and beyond Gloria's control. The more she thought, the more confusion muddled her brain. The best idea was simply to play things by ear—no more being forward. "Play it cool" would be her motto. That would be so hard to do!

Wonder of wonders, Ben did contact Gloria and verified a specific time and date for their shopping adventure. In fact he sent another e-mail to remind her of the time and date at his place.

Gloria/Bobette was excited and hoped it would be like old times. Well, it wasn't like that at all. The sex was rushed, and Ben had forgotten to take his Viagra. Bobette did not stay as long as usual. Ben hadn't eaten dinner, and she wanted to get home before dark. What a complete waste of anticipation. They didn't have their relaxing and wonderful time on the patio chatting about this and that.

A few weeks passed. Ben did keep in contact but only to tell Bobette about his dear friend whom he was so very close with and had worked with him through the years on many different projects, even writing a book on different religions. Ben's friend had suddenly had a severe heart attack and was placed in intensive care at Denver General Hospital. Tests were run; everything possible was being done for Rudolph Lee Orson, known as Rudy. His condition was so uncertain. Ben spent all of his time with the family and at the hospital. The family had talked about pulling the plug. Poor Rudy had been on a life support system for a week. Only the family was allowed to visit. Ben was a total basket case by that time.

Bobette wanted to console him, but he was never at home. He was at the hospital; even though he wasn't allowed. Only the immediate family was allowed. Ben didn't eat and didn't indulge in any of the favorite activities that were his life. All he did was mope. He managed to get very sick with a sore throat and a congested chest.

Gloria looked at the Gemini horoscope in the day's paper thinking it possibly could be of some help. It read:

> Your interest in love may be getting complex as the days go by, leaving you somewhat unsatisfied. The problem is that your gratification will come only from the deeper emotional waters now, and your fears may keep you from diving in. It's time to be brave, Gemini, and to delve beneath the light and easy surface.

That was a thought to be pondered. It seemed right on the money.

Ben did not show his usual charming personality. His only thoughts were of his best friend, Rudy. They had been compadres for a very long time and were almost like brothers.

Although Ben had a lot of friends, Gloria thought it was strange that when she was at his house, nobody; not even one time, came to see him when the two of them were frolicking in the bedroom. One might say it was uncanny.

Gloria mulled the situation over in her mind. Things were impossible. At least she should have been able to visit Ben and give him some consolation as a very good friend and not his playmate. This thought kept running through her head. *Should she or shouldn't she?* Gloria was truly worried about Ben and very concerned.

A few hours passed. Gloria was sure Ben would not notify his family of Rudy's condition. He was not close to anyone in his family. Gloria did not know why but wished in the worst way that she did. Figuring Ben out was impossible. He was a man of mystery!

The decision was made. She had to see him. This situation had to be solved. Gloria, in a fit of desperation, telephoned him.

"Hello," Ben answered.

"Hello Ben, may I come over just for a few minutes? I need to see you!"

"Yes."

Gloria was on her way. She was going to give him the biggest hug. Oh how she had missed him!

She arrived quickly. Her heart was beating so quickly. She had missed Ben terribly and was going to try to console him, not to pressure him into sex.

Ben wasn't waiting at the back gate as usual. Bobette unfastened the gate, and there was Ben sitting in a chair with a sweater and a big purple cap on, talking earnestly on the phone. He did not acknowledge her at all, but his dog did. Bobette sat down in a chair. The dog, Major, jumped up on her lap and started giving her big kisses. Major had never done that before. He was giving Bobette a fantastic welcome although it had been a long time since he had seen her. Well, at least Major loved her!

Ben kept on talking, still not looking at Bobette or waving a hand at her. He was smoking. Ben got up and walked through the sliding doors, still yakking on the phone, and sat down on the couch in the living room. The talking went on and on. Bobette became more than just plain irritated. She jumped up out of her chair and went into the kitchen. She wrapped up the egg-salad sandwich she had brought him and put it into his fridge. She left a can of asparagus soup on the counter. Quickly she wrote a note: "I have to go." She waved good-bye to Ben. He did not wave back or bother to look at her.

Bobette was so sad by that time. *It'll be a rainy day in hell before I ever come back here*, she thought.

Later that day Gloria turned on the computer. An e-mail from Ben read, "Friends?" It also said that Rudy's wife, Maria, had phoned Ben an hour ago to advise him that her husband, Rudy, had passed away at 7:00 p.m.

Gloria was numb. Why had this happened? It just couldn't be! Now what was going to happen to Ben? He had not been himself ever since Rudy had the heart attack.

It was the day of the funeral. The sun did not shine. It was cloudy and a bit rainy.

Gloria wondered if she'd ever hear from Ben again. It seemed to her that he was much more depressed over losing Rudy than he had been about losing his longtime partner. Rudy's demise had been unexpected, and Olivia's could have been a relief. Being a caretaker was one of the most difficult jobs in the world for anyone.

Gloria still could not comprehend Ben's treatment of her. In her mind, she asked the question, *What could Ben possibly like better than wonderful sex?* Why was her brain interfering with reality? Ben had said, "I don't want sex now. I just don't want it!"

He started e-mailing Gloria now and then again. What a surprise. He was one hard José to figure out. The excitement just wasn't there anymore. What to do, what to do! Nothing—the ball was in Ben's court. One e-mail consisted of how to keep your computer clean, the amazing effects of eating a banana each day, and funny little jokes—nothing too titillating. Where had all the fun and excitement gone?

Time passed. Life had definitely changed. Gloria sent Ben e-mails now and then, telling him how worried she was about him and asking if there was anything she could do for him. There was never a reply—never.

Gloria simply just gave up, thinking that she had to be the biggest fool in the entire universe. If Ben preferred to wallow in self-pity, well then, so be it.

Several months passed, but one day there was a message on the computer from Ben. Was Gloria seeing things? She was in a daze as she read his words. Ben actually had the nerve to invite her to his place for whatever. He apologized for ignoring her attempts to see him or have a talk on the telephone.

Bobette accepted his invitation. What was this stranglehold he had over her? Why didn't she ignore him like he had her? Why didn't she make him grovel or behave obsequiously?

The two of them met at the black-iron gate. Ben opened it and grabbed Bobette in his arms. No words were spoken. Conversation was not needed at that moment. Ben then took Bobette's hand and led her into the small kitchen, locking the sliding glass door and closing the drapes. Ben gave Bobette another hug, took her hand, and led her upstairs to the bedroom. Still no words were spoken. While undressing there was the usual procedure of fondling and rubbing their hot bodies against one another, then into the shower they went with more fondling and sexual foreplay. After toweling off, to the bed they went. Bobette did not notice the color of the sheets this time. Who cared?

Ben crawled on top of her and looked into her very blue eyes. "Darling, I have a fantasy!"

"What is it?"

Ben slipped a pillow underneath Bobette's head, climbed on top of her, and gently inserted his partially erect penis right into her delicate mouth. No complaints were uttered. He began pumping up and down harder and harder. Ben was going fast and furiously, enjoying every delicious moment of it.

Bobette thought she may not have a mouth or throat by the time this ordeal was complete. When Ben climaxed, he trembled like an oncoming earthquake.

This was not romantic. It wasn't anything—no candlelight or soft music. What was it? Did it really matter? Ben did not even say, "Thank you."

There was no sitting out on the patio although it was cool, no hugs or kisses good-bye, no cheerful chats, no anything.

As the disillusioned Bobette was leaving, Ben said, "I'll keep in touch."

That literally was the lie of the century. They never saw one another again.

Chapter 28

Unbelievable Irony

Two entire years had gone by. Not one word from Ben. He simply did not acknowledge any of Gloria's e-mails, even when she wished him a special happy birthday. Nothing. What kind of a man was he anyway? When an affair is over, shouldn't it be acknowledged with a few kind words, not just leaving one hanging in midair, wondering what really had happened or hadn't happened?

Gloria had saved many of his e-mails. She came by an old one:

> Just by way of defending myself—and I seem to do a lot of that with you—tomorrow the cleaning folks are coming; tomorrow night I have my regular coffee with the club; on Thursday Leslie's son is marrying; I'm anticipating visits from one or two of Olivia's other kids from out of town; I'm attending the wedding reception/luncheon following the ceremony; I had already arranged to do camera stuff with another daughter and her husband on Friday; and so on and so on.
>
> Call me a butterfly if you wish. If all this is off-putting to you, well, there it is.

Ben certainly had been busy after Olivia's death. Gloria had always called him "the butterfly of the zodiac" when they had first met. He had many obligations and social get-togethers. In truth he was a social butterfly.

Many times Gloria thought she should just show up on Ben's doorstep. The element of surprise might shock him into reality. One day she would undoubtedly do just that. No rush; it had been such a long time since they had been together. The fact that Gloria did not know a single friend of Ben's was not helpful. She would like to know how he was doing, and was he working or retired? So many unanswered questions. Why couldn't she get Ben out of her mind? He was always in her dreams but trying to escape from her. Maybe things would have turned out differently if she had not been the aggressor and worn her heart on her sleeve.

Getting back to reality had to be a necessity. Gloria needed to get her obsession with Ben out of her head completely. The ennui of the situation was destroying her common sense. It was not like her to have time on her hands. As a close-knit family, there was always an activity or birthday to be celebrated. Richard and Gloria had several favorite television programs they watched. Then there was the computer. Richard commented that his wife had become addicted to it. He was not happy about that and wished he had never bought the damn thing. He thought housework would be a better thing to do.

It had taken time to learn about the computer. Gloria's girls would often come over to help their mother when it stopped working. They were so knowledgeable. There were also the technicians who could be gotten by phone. Solitaire was a game to be played on the computer. It was fun; it made one never want to play the game with cards. Scrabble was another thing to play. Gloria hadn't mastered that yet.

Time passed as it has a habit of doing. Gloria often stood at the kitchen window looking outside. She and her neighbor across the street kept an eye on each other's house. It was just a habit but a good one. Today was a beautiful day. The trees were starting to bloom and a few flowers. The birds were singing cheerfully. Some of the neighbors' dogs were tearing up and down the street. They were happy to escape from their fenced-in yards.

Gloria wished she was that happy. She should definitely take the time to smell the roses and count her blessings. Instead of doing that, she strolled over to her dear computer and turned it on. This morning Gloria had neglected to read the newspaper. That was unusual because, after Richard would leave for work, that was the first thing to be done—housework would have to take second place. Life was not hectic these days with just the two of them and not seven. Yes, life was serene and fairly quiet. It was a wonder Richard and Gloria had managed to raise their family and still remain of sound mind. Yes, there were trials and tribulations.

At that time in life, Gloria and Richard had numerous grandchildren and weren't asking for more. On the other hand, their friends were begging for grandchildren, and it did not happen. Life is not always fair. However, all's fair in love and war.

It was the usual uninteresting politics and shootings that seemed to dominate the news. As a preference Gloria turned on her computer every time the family had departed for the day. By that time she had become addicted to it.

All of a sudden she sat straight up in her chair. The computer words did not make sense! She read them again. It was not today's news. It was old, from last week. The words seemed to magnify before her bewildered eyes. It read: "Benjamin J. Carter, well-known social worker, speaker, and author, died a week ago." It went on and on about his numerous and generous contributions to society. His wish was to have no obituary and no funeral.

Gloria screamed in disbelief, "This is not true! It must be some kind of a sick joke!" She was the only one at home, and her screams were so violent. She just sat there for a full ten minutes with her head hung low and her eyes closed. There must have been a mistake. She stared at the words again, "Benjamin J. Carter, well-known social worker, speaker, and author died a week ago. He was loved by many and will be sorely missed." Gloria could not read the article in its entirety. She did read that his wishes were to be cremated and scattered around his favorite places. This was unbelievable—not even a grave to visit and mourn.

Gloria was not only sad but mad—mad as a hornet's nest. Why, why, why hadn't Ben had the human decency to contact her? Why hadn't he left her a letter or something of remembrance? The whys and wherefores were too overwhelming—worse than a terrible nightmare.

Much later that day, Gloria found online two different newspapers that had quite elegant stories about Ben: the *Denver Post* and the *Rocky Mountain News*. It was, as a rule, customary to read the *Denver Post*. It was a complete mystery as to why this gigantic news had passed her by. Gloria made a print of everything online about Ben. Her printer was doing an excellent job. The words she read were unbelievable. Why, Ben was famous! He had been loved by many and helped many aspiring authors. There were two pictures of Ben in each newspaper. Gloria was not dreaming. Almost out of her mind, the printed information was put away in a safe place. Ben was famous. Why didn't she know it? She thought she had known him. The ironic part was that she hadn't known him at all—just in bed!

A week passed. Those dreadful articles were read and reread time after time. By a miracle one of Ben's close friends was named. After much research Gloria found the phone number of this close friend, George Childs. She telephoned him immediately. The phone rang and rang. Patience was not one of Gloria's virtues. Finally an automated voice said, "If this is a solicitor, please hang up and put this on your 'do not call' list. Otherwise, stay on the line."

Gloria waited impatiently. Finally a voice answered, "Hello."

"Hello, is this Mr. George Childs?"

"Yes, yes it is."

By that time Gloria was in tears. "I am a friend of Ben's, and I am absolutely devastated about his death. I had no idea he had been sick."

What can I do to help you?"

"Just talk to me. Tell me about Ben. I simply cannot believe he is gone. I can't! I should've died before he did. I am ten years older. I don't know even one of his friends. Did you know him well?"

"I knew him pretty well. Everybody seemed to like him a great deal."

Still crying, Gloria continued, "I know that. I do know he was always helping friends. He told me he couldn't help himself though."

Mr. Childs was very sympathetic. "How long did you know him?"

"At least thirty-five years. I thought I knew him inside and out. The sad thing is I did not know him at all. I didn't get to tell him good-bye. That was so wrong!"

Gloria was thinking that perhaps Mr. Childs perceived her as a fool. He actually didn't. He was very interested in the conversation.

"Can you call me again sometime?" he asked. "My wife is just coming in the door."

"Okay. Thank you for letting me cry on your shoulder."

Gloria did not know if she would call again or not. The circumstances did not seem to be real. How could she exist now that the love of her life was gone forever? This thought kept running through her mind. There was absolutely no one at all that she could confide in about this situation—no one at all. Then there could be the possibility of blackmail. What to do, what to do? There was not a single soul to tell or ask for advice.

Wallowing in self-pity was not a positive thing. It was time to put the crying towel away. A brilliant idea popped into Gloria's fried brain. There was one person who knew about Ben and her affair. Of course—Dr. Brahms. Would he still be in Denver? The telephone book was of no help. When all else fails, rely on the trusty computer! It seemed to have a mind of its own. After a very long time, five names appeared, but all the very same. Gloria's determination had paid off. She called every one of them; most of them thought she was as loony as a jaybird. Finally her persistence persevered. Nervously the telephone number was dialed. It rang and rang forever; then an answering machine came on.

"This is Dr. Brahms. Leave me your name and number. I will get back to you."

That would not have been a smart thing to do. Richard must not know about this. No doubt her phone number would be on Dr. Brahms's caller ID. Worry, worry, worry. Gloria hung up the phone. After some thought she called the number back and left a message on Dr. Brahms's answering machine.

"This is Gloria Madsen from Denver. I hope you remember me from years and years ago. Please don't return my call. It would be a complete disaster if my husband heard us talking. I will call you again."

Later that day more calls were made to Dr. Brahms. The same message was repeated: "This is Dr. Brahms. Give me your number. I will return your call."

Was Dr. Brahms ever in his office? The next day Gloria was finally successful in getting him. It took him by surprise; he had some difficulty in remembering Ben and Gloria. It had been such a long time since he had left Denver to move to California. Gloria mentioned several incidents to refresh his memory. He seemed old and not the young upstart he had been when Gloria first had met him. They talked for a short time. Gloria poured out her heart and soul to him while crying between sentences. The shrink seemed quite distant and would offer no help. All he could say was, "You need help. You need help! I can refer you to—"

"Stop, Dr. Brahms!" Gloria said. "I don't need help. Remember that you always told me how resilient I was? Well, I still am. I still am. I don't need help from anybody! I just want your honest opinion of Ben. How could he treat me like this and just disappear from my life with no sense whatsoever of some kind of a closure? Why couldn't he have told me good-bye, nice knowing you?"

There were a few moments of complete silence. Dr. Brahms then spoke in a loud voice, "He's a *bum*."

What a shock to hear those words. Gloria couldn't believe what he had said! She forgot to ask the rest of the questions that were on her mind. In disbelief she hung up the phone without saying another word. This strange statement required serious thought.

After pondering Dr. Brahms's dreadful words, Gloria arrived at the unbelievable decision that he could have been correct. Perhaps Ben's friend, George Childs, would have a better perspective on the situation than the psychiatrist. Was it worth a try? Yes, definitely. At her wits' end, Gloria found Mr. Child's phone number where it was hidden, neatly folded inside her precious jewelry box.

Trembling, she slowly dialed, wondering if she was doing the right thing. There was an answering machine: "If this is a solicitor, please hang up and put this number on your 'do not call' list. Otherwise stay on the line."

After a few long moments, someone answered. "Hello."

"Hello, Mr. Childs?" Gloria asked.

"This is he. How may I help you?"

"This is Gloria again. May I have a few moments of your time?"

"Of course."

"I am so sorry to bother you again, but I just can't believe that Ben is gone. Please, please tell me about him."

"He was a very outgoing person and was into social work."

"I know that. In reality. I didn't know too much about him—mostly the information he gave when he was a communicastor on the radio talk show. He had so many admirers. I believe I was his greatest admirer."

"You know that Ben had been very sick for a couple of months?"

"No, no, I didn't know that at all until I read it online. I can't even go to his grave to mourn. He had no funeral and had his ashes spread heaven knows where. I simply can't understand his actions. I hate myself for not going to see him. I hate him for not letting me know his condition. I am inclined to think Ben was quite the ladies' man!"

'Yes, Gloria, I believe he was. Were you and he romantically inclined?"

"Yes, yes we were."

"Ben did tell me about a woman with whom he was involved, and he said he was sorry for the way he had treated her. He said he loved her."

"Oh, oh, that could've been me! That must've been me! What was her name?"

"He didn't say."

Gloria sighed. "I thought he was going to be an organ donor. It was not mentioned in the articles I read about him."

"He was a mess. So many things were wrong with him. His body was rejected."

"That's hard to believe. He was such a health nut."

"Gloria, maybe we can meet sometime, have a cup of coffee, and talk some more about Ben."

"I'd really like that, Mr. Childs. When spring comes. Nice weather would be better."

The nice weather finally arrived. Gloria telephoned Mr. Childs; his wife answered, and Gloria asked, "Is Mr. Maurice there?"

"I think you have the wrong number."

"I am so sorry. I must have misdialed."

The next day Gloria called again, and Mr. Childs was not at home; no one was there.

Another day passed. Maybe the third try would be a charm. It had to be. It was not though. Mr. Childs was not at home again. It was time to give up. Besides, maybe Mr. Childs had an ulterior motive. Humph! No one could ever take Ben's place. Nobody!

Gloria never stopped thinking about how and wondering why Ben had tossed her aside like an old worn-out shoe. She had always put him on the highest pedestal and felt so special and grateful that he had let her into his life. How many women were in his life? Only God knew the answer.

There was an article in the paper about broken hearts, saying they could cause considerable damage. When a loved one was lost, it was like a heart attack. The medical term was *stress cardiomyopathy*. Symptoms were chest pain and shortness of breath. Forget that; Gloria was resilient. She did have the symptom of not being able to sleep.

Mr. Childs had told her about many of Ben's negative qualities that seemed unreal, and Gloria wondered why he had told her if he were a good friend.

Three long years passed. A letter from Ben did not happen and was never going to happen. Why was hope kept alive? Gloria could still heard the words of Dr. Brahms ringing in her ears: "He's a *bum.*"

Would Gloria ever be able to forget this wretched trauma and put it completely out of her mind? It took several long years for her to write the book *No Good-Bye.* Each word that was written was a painful reminder of the past. There were also the beautiful times that gladdened her heart almost as if she were living them over again. She was hopeful that she had become a better woman for this unbelievable romantic yet devastating experience and that she would ultimately lead a more Christian life in her remaining years. She had to believe the words of Dr. Brahms, who said she was resilient, and of a former neighbor who had told her she had nerves of steel.

What about retribution? It was a certainty that Gloria would be punished for her sinful association with Ben over three decades.

There was a little card in Gloria's purse lying on the table that was trying to fall out. She picked it up. There was a beautiful picture of Jesus on it with these words below:

> Amen, Amen.
> I say to you,
> he who
> hears my word
> and believes
> he who
> sent me has
> life everlasting
> and does not come
> to judgment
> but has passed
> from
> death to life.
> —John 5:24

For several long moments, Gloria desperately wanted to believe these words of God. Could they be true?

On second thought Gloria transformed into Bobette for the last time and muttered under her breath, “How could you leave me without saying good-bye? How could you? How could you? Well, this is no good-bye! You will meet your little vixen again; be it in heaven or in hell or in reincarnation!”

d at www.ICGtesting.com

12/P

9 781492 276

CPSIA information can be obtaine
Printed in the USA
LVOW04s0329010914
401751LV00020B/7

CPSIA information can be obtained at www.ICGtesting.com
Printed in the USA
LVOW04s0329010914

401751LV00020B/712/P